"I Need Company."

Patrina studied Cole's expression, searching his eyes for some clue to his meaning. "Company?"

"Yes, company. I don't like eating alone," Cole said.

Patrina had a sinking feeling. He didn't know her and there was a lot she didn't know about him. But one thing was certain—the sizzling, sexual chemistry flowing between them. And yet, the last thing on her agenda was getting involved in an affair destined to go nowhere. Besides, Cole Westmoreland was a *lawman*.

She glanced at Cole and saw a sexy smile curve his lips and a twinkle spark in his dark-brown eyes. The man was messing with her rational mind, and making it difficult for her to breathe.

"It looks like we're stuck here together," he said, glancing out the window. At that moment, Patrina realized that whether she liked it or not, she was temporarily stranded with Cole Westmoreland.

Dear Reader,

From the moment I introduced Dr. Patrina Foreman in *The Durango Affair,* I knew I had just the man to heal her mourning heart. What she needed was a take-charge man. A man of action. A man like Cole Westmoreland.

Being the quintessential Westmoreland male that he is, Cole was just out to have a short, sizzling love affair while visiting his family in Montana. He was a man who could read a woman like a book and he was reading interest in Patrina's eyes. A good dose of lovemaking was just what the good doctor should be ordering to kick-start her life all over again. And he intended to give the term "merry widow" a whole new meaning.

What Cole didn't count on was learning a hard lesson on how to differentiate lust from love. In the end he discovered what he really needed was Patrina as part of his life—for always.

I hope all of you enjoy reading Cole and Patrina's story as much as I enjoyed writing it.

Happy Reading!

Brenda Jackson

BRENDA JACKSON

COLE'S RED-HOT PURSUIT

Silhouette® Desire

Published by Silhouette Books
America's Publisher of Contemporary Romance

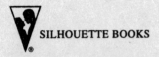 SILHOUETTE BOOKS

ISBN-13: 978-0-373-76874-5
ISBN-10:   0-373-76874-5

COLE'S RED-HOT PURSUIT

BRENDA JACKSON

is a die "heart" romantic who married her childhood sweetheart and still proudly wears the "going steady" ring he gave her when she was fifteen. Because she's always believed in the power of love, Brenda's stories always have happy endings. In her real-life love story, Brenda and her husband of thirty-three years live in Jacksonville, Florida, and have two sons.

A *USA TODAY* bestselling author of more than fifty romance titles, Brenda is a recent retiree who worked thirty-seven years in management at a major insurance company. She divides her time between family, writing and traveling with Gerald. You may write Brenda at P.O. Box 28267, Jacksonville, FL 32226, by e-mail at WriterBJackson@aol.com or visit her Web site at www.brendajackson.net.

To the love of my life, Gerald Jackson, Sr.

To all former coworkers at State Farm Insurance.
Retirement is fun but I miss you guys!

Many waters cannot quench love;
rivers cannot wash it away.

—*Song of Solomon* 8:7

Prologue

"I swear, Cole, if you weren't so preoccupied with staring at Patrina Foreman, you would have noticed that McKinnon was about to knock the hell out of Rick Summers just now for coming on to your sister," Durango Westmoreland said, joining his cousin near the punch bowl.

"Who?" Cole asked, finally taking his eyes off the woman across the room, the same one he'd been standing here watching since she'd arrived at the party given in honor of his sister, Casey.

"Rick Summers. He's been a pain in the—"

"No, I'm not talking about Summers. I'm talking about the woman. You said her name was Patrina..."

Durango shook his head, clearly seeing his cousin's interest. "Her name is Patrina Foreman, but those who know her call her Trina. She's a doctor in town. In fact, she's Savannah's doctor and will be delivering the baby."

"Married?"

"She's a widow. Her husband, Perry, was the sheriff and was gunned down by an escaped convict almost three years ago. Trina and Perry had been childhood sweethearts so she took his death pretty hard."

Durango didn't say anything for a few minutes and then said, "If you're thinking what I think you're thinking, you might want to kill the thought. You're a Texas Ranger and Trina has sworn never to become involved with another lawman. Hell, to be totally honest, she hasn't done too much dating at all. Other than her work, Trina's life basically stopped when Perry died."

Cole immediately thought, *what a waste*. Patrina Foreman was a looker. She'd certainly grabbed his attention the moment she'd walked in the room. He couldn't recall the last time something so potent had happened between him and a woman. And there was no way he would let the party end without at least getting an introduction—especially when he'd felt the strong sexual chemistry between them when their gazes had caught and held. There was no way she hadn't felt it, as well, he was sure of it. And would even go so far as to place his ranger's badge on it.

"I think I'll go introduce myself."

Durango rolled his eyes on seeing the determined look on Cole's face. "Okay, but don't say I didn't warn you."

A smooth smile touched Cole's lips when he glanced back over at Patrina and caught her staring at him. "I won't."

One

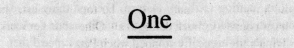

Eleven months later

It seemed to require more effort than usual for Cole Westmoreland to open his eyes, and the moment he did, he wished he'd kept them closed. A sharp pain ripped through his body, starting at the top of his head and working its way down to the soles of his feet. To fight off the excruciating throb he tightened his hands into fists, and then it occurred to him that he was lying flat on his back in the middle of a bed that wasn't his.

He forced himself to gaze around a bedroom that wasn't his, either. In fact, he was at a loss as to whose bedroom it was. He closed his eyes against another sharp pain and wondered just where the hell he was.

He recalled getting off the plane at the Bozeman

Airport and renting a car to drive to his sister and brother-in-law's home on the outskirts of town. Casey and McKinnon weren't expecting him for another three weeks. His early arrival was to have been a surprise. He also remembered dismissing the car rental office's warning that an April snowstorm was headed their way. He'd assumed he would reach his destination before the storm hit.

But he had been wrong.

He'd been driving the rental car along the two-lane highway when out of nowhere, blankets of snow began falling, cutting visibility to zero. The last thing he remembered was tightening his grip on the steering wheel when he felt himself losing control of the car and then mouthing a curse before hitting something.

He reopened his eyes when he heard a sound. He forced his head to move, and his gaze locked on to the woman who entered the bedroom. *She definitely isn't my sister, Casey, so who is she?* He watched her place a basket of clothes on a table near the fireplace, and when she began folding up the clothes he studied her face.

She looked familiar and he searched his mind, trying to recall where he'd seen her before. He was not one to forget an attractive face, and even while flat on his back with pain racking his body, he was male enough to appreciate a pretty woman when he saw one.

And she was pretty.

She was tall. He figured her to be at least five-ten, and to his way of thinking, one gorgeous Amazon who could certainly complement his six-four. Her dark hair was pulled back in a ponytail. Her cocoa-brown face had

high cheekbones, a pert nose—full lips that caught his
gaze in a mesmerizing hold. He seemed to recall that
he'd gazed at those same lips before and had gotten the
same gut-wrenching reaction. Suddenly his stomach
clenched in recognition.

Patrina Foreman.

They had met last year at a party given in his sister's
honor by his stepmother, Abby, and McKinnon's mother,
Morning Star. He and his brother, Clint, had flown in
from Texas for the affair. Cole distinctly remembered
how Patrina had kicked his libido into gear that night
when he'd first seen her. The very air he'd been breathing had seemed to get snatched right from his lungs the
moment their eyes had met. And then when his gaze had
scanned her full-figured body, he'd been a goner. He
was a man who appreciated a woman with some meat
on her body, and Patrina's voluptuousness had been like
an exploding bomb, sending all kinds of sensations rock-
eting through him.

According to his cousin, Durango, she was twenty-
eight, and since he'd said that close to a year ago, she
was probably twenty-nine now. And his cousin had also
told him that Patrina was the gynecologist in town, and
that she had lost her husband a few years back. A sheriff,
her husband had died in the line of duty.

He'd also seen her in November at Casey and Mc-
Kinnon's wedding, although she'd left before he'd gotten a chance to say anything to her. But the heated
chemistry had still been there, even from across the
room.

He continued to watch her fold the clothes and couldn't

help wondering why he was lying flat on his back on a bed in her home. He moved his mouth to ask, but no sound came forth. Instead, for some reason he didn't quite understand, he suddenly felt tired. The next thing he knew, he was succumbing to darkness once more.

Patrina Foreman hummed softly as she folded the last of her clothes. She took a sidelong glance at the man sleeping in her guest-room bed and noted he was still asleep. If he didn't wake up pretty soon, she would have to wake him and check his vital signs again. It was sheer luck that she'd come along Craven Road when she had; otherwise, no telling how long he would have remained in that car, unconscious. And with the weather as it was, she didn't want to think about what might have happened.

Once she'd seen that his injuries were minor, although the force of the impact had literally knocked him out, she'd managed to bring him around long enough to get him out of his vehicle and into hers. And then when she'd reached her ranch, it had been quite a challenge to get him into the house, since he wasn't exactly a small man. By taking advantage of the moments he regained consciousness, she'd managed to coax him into doing whatever she asked—like stripping down to his boxers and getting into bed under plenty of blankets to stay warm. She seriously doubted he would remember any of it, but she was certain it was something *she* would never forget.

She hadn't averted her gaze quickly enough and had seen his manly physique before he'd slipped beneath the covers. She had been nearly overtaken by emotions she couldn't even begin to name, emotions she hadn't had to deal with in quite some time. For as long as she lived, she wouldn't forget the sight of his broad shoulders, taut hips and long, masculine legs. She'd been shocked at how the fire of desire had flickered across every inch of her skin, and how her breath had gotten lodged in her throat.

She'd recognized him the moment she'd opened the door to his car to find him slumped over the steering wheel. Cole Westmoreland, a Texas Ranger who was related to all the other Westmorelands living around these parts. He was Corey Westmoreland's son, Casey Westmoreland Quinn's brother and Durango Westmoreland's cousin. She also knew he was a triplet to Casey and their brother, Clint, whom she'd heard had recently gotten married.

Because the roads were blocked and getting help for Cole would have been next to impossible, she'd made the decision to bring him here. So far he'd been an easy-going patient. It had been five hours since she'd gotten him settled. She figured that pretty soon he would wake up, if for nothing other than to go to the bathroom. And just in case he was hungry, she'd fixed a pot of beef stew.

She glanced out the window. The snow was still falling heavily. The phones lines were down and she could not get a signal on her cell phone. The battery-operated radio in the kitchen said it would be another two days before things let up. It was one of those rare blizzards these parts were prone to in April. While most of the country was enjoying beautiful spring weather, Bozeman, Montana, was still in the clutches of what had been a nasty winter. So at the moment the two of them were stranded here at her ranch. She was glad she'd taken a week off work—with no babies due to arrive this month, she'd planned to spend her time reading and relaxing. She hadn't counted on having a visitor.

Suddenly she felt an elemental change in the air that had nothing to do with the weather. And then she heard the sound of her name, a whisper so soft it caressed her skin and almost made her shiver. She looked across the room and found her gaze trapped with Cole Westmoreland's.

For an endless moment she stared into the dark depths of his eyes before pulling in a deep breath. This very thing had happened the first time she'd seen him last year at a party given for his sister. It seemed that the moment she'd entered the room that night his gaze had connected to hers and held. Now he was looking at her in a way she'd figured she would never experience again. And her response to his stare was affecting her in a way she wasn't prepared for.

"Water."

His request had her moving across the room to him and the pitcher that sat beside the bed. She tried ignoring the way he was looking at her while she poured him a glass of water. And then she placed her hand behind his head for support while he took a sip, and tried not to notice how warm he felt. He didn't have a fever. If anyone did it was her. She could feel her body get hot and tingly.

This was the first man she'd been attracted to since Perry's death. She had dated but not on a regular basis, and none of the men had stirred her the way Cole West-moreland had done before and was doing now. His gaze was sweeping slowly across her face, and to her way of thinking, it shifted and zeroed in on her lips and stayed there.

"Do you want more?" she asked after he had drained the entire glass.

His gaze returned to her eyes. "No, and thanks."

His deep, raspy voice floated across her nerve endings. Trying to retain control of her mind and senses, she eased his head back onto the pillow while trying to avoid thinking about the large, masculine body beneath the blanket. Even with the blanket's thickness she could make out his long, hard limbs. Elemental. Powerful. Male.

"Why am I here?" he asked, causing her to shift her gaze and look at him.

She lifted his wrist to take his pulse and could feel how erratically her own was beating. "Don't you remember?"

"No," he said simply.

That wasn't unusual and she nodded. "You were in a car accident and took a bump to the head."

"And how did I get here?"

"I came across you on my way home. I figured you must have been trying to make it to Casey and McKinnon's place before the storm hit. You're lucky I came along when I did."

"Was I unconscious?"

"Just about," she said, returning his arm to his side, satisfied with his pulse rate but not with the way he was still staring at her mouth. "I was able to get you to cooperate, which is how I managed to get you out of the car and into mine. The same thing when I arrived here. Although you had to lean on me, I was able to manage you pretty well."

She couldn't help but smile when she said, "I was even able to get you to take off your clothes on your own and get into bed."

Cole nodded. He could believe that, since he'd never had a problem with taking off his clothes for any woman, and she definitely would not have been an exception. But he found it hard to believe that she alone had managed to get him in and out of her car. She wasn't a tiny woman, but compared to him, she was a lightweight. He was all solid and she was all soft curves.

"How long have I been here?" he decided to ask, not needing to dwell on her shape and size any longer.

"About five hours. You've been going in and out most of the time, but you've slept rather comfortably over the past couple of hours or so. But eventually I was going to have to wake you. When you take a hit on the head it's not good to sleep too much."

He nodded again, thinking, so he'd been told. There were two doctors in the Westmoreland family—his cousin Delaney and his cousin Thorn's wife, Tara.

"Are you hungry?"

He glanced up at her. "No. Thanks for asking," he said. He then glanced around the room.

"Power is out. I have a generator, so we have electricity, but the phone lines are down and the signal for the cell phone is nonexistent. I don't have any way to let Casey or your father know you're here and all right."

His gaze returned to hers. "That's fine. Neither she nor Dad was expecting me for another three weeks, anyway. I was going to surprise them."

Patrina nodded. Casey lived a few miles down the

road as did Durango and his wife, Savannah. Patrina had delivered their baby last September, a beautiful little girl they had named Sarah after Durango's mother. And Cole's father, Corey, lived on what everyone in these parts referred to as Corey's Mountain. She rarely saw Corey these days unless he and his wife, Abby, came down to visit their good friends, Morning Star and Martin Quinn, McKinnon's parents. But she usually ran into Casey at least once a week in town or just passing on the road.

"I've changed my mind."

His words intruded into her thoughts. She met his gaze and tried not to drown in the dark depths. She thought he had such beautiful eyes. She licked her lips. They seemed to go dry around him from some reason. Probably from her heated breath. "About what?"

"Food. I'm feeling hungry."

"Okay. I'll bring you some stew I've made."

"I can get up," he mumbled. "I'm not an invalid." Cole didn't like the thought of anyone, especially a woman, waiting on him. He felt fine. So fine that he'd almost slipped and said he was feeling horny, instead of hungry. Hell, just being this close to her had his heart thudding hard against his ribs, and had other parts of him throbbing.

"I would prefer that you didn't get up, Cole. You should stay put for a while. I checked you over and didn't feel any broken bones."

He lifted a brow. She'd checked him over? Hmm, he wondered if she'd felt something else besides no broken bones. As if she'd read his mind she quickly said. "I am a medical doctor, you know."

He couldn't help the smile that touched his lips. "You deliver babies and take care of womenfolk, right?"

"Yes, but that doesn't mean I can't take care of a man if I have to," she said as she turned to leave the room.

He couldn't help but chuckle at her tone. "Ah, that's good to know. I'm definitely going to remember that."

She glanced back over her shoulder. "Remember what?"

"That you can take care of a man."

The look she threw his way indicated he better be nice or else. And at that moment, he couldn't help wondering what that *or else* was.

Annoyed with herself for letting Cole rile her, Patrina moved around the kitchen to prepare him something to eat. The beef stew had been simmering and its aroma filled the kitchen.

Because she had grown up in these parts and was used to the cold, harsh winters, she was never caught unawares. She made sure her freezer and cupboards were always full, and she had installed the generator a few years back.

As she loaded a tray for Cole, she tried to recall the last time a man had stayed overnight in her home. It probably was last year when her brother, Dale, had come in from Phoenix to attend McKinnon's wedding. At the same time she and Perry had been sweethearts, Dale and Perry had grown up in Bozeman the best of friends. More than once Dale had reminded Patrina that Perry had always said if anything ever happened to him, he would not want her to mourn him but, rather, have a rich and fulfilling life. She wished it could be that easy, but it wasn't. More times than not she went to bed missing the love she had lost.

A few minutes later she walked through the house and headed toward the bedroom carrying a tray loaded with food. In addition to the beef stew, she had made him a turkey sandwich and had also included a slice of the chocolate cake she had baked earlier in the week.

When she walked into the room she wasn't surprised to find the bed empty, even though she had asked him to stay put. Until she was certain he could move around on his own, she had wanted to be there to help him. The last thing she needed was for him to have a dizzy spell and fall.

The sound of running water confirmed her suspicions. He was taking a shower. She tried to force from her mind the image of him standing without any clothes on beneath a spray of water. She didn't know what was wrong with her. She didn't usually have such wanton thoughts. She was a doctor, a professional, but ever since she'd looked up to see Cole staring at her with those intense dark eyes of his, she'd been reminded that she was also a woman. He'd looked at her the same way that night last year at Casey's party. And the heat of his gaze had affected her in a way she hadn't been used to, and she'd quickly made the decision that Cole Westmoreland was someone she should steer clear of. In addition to being a man who could turn her life topsy-turvy if given the chance, she had also learned he was a lawman, and after Perry's death, she had vowed never to become involved with a lawman again.

"I was hoping to make it back to bed before you returned."

Patrina turned around and wished she hadn't. Cole stood in the doorway of the bathroom with a sheepish grin on his face. But what really caught her attention was the fact that he was completely naked, except for the towel around his middle. Of their own accord, her eyes raked his body. Why did he have to be so fine? So well built? She could just imagine running her hands over those hard muscular planes and—"

"The food smells good."

It occurred to her that she'd been standing there staring at him. She immediately dropped her eyes from his body and automatically licked her lips. "Well, since you're up and about, I'll leave this tray in here for you. There're also two pills for pain. You might not think you're hurting now, but you may experience some discomfort now that you've started moving around."

"Aren't you going to eat?"

What I'm going to do is get out of here before I do something real stupid, like cross the room and touch you to see if all those muscles are as hard as they look. "No, I have a couple of things to do in the kitchen. Go ahead and enjoy your meal." She turned to leave the room.

"Patrina?"

She turned back around before reaching the door. She met his gaze. "Yes?"

"Thanks for everything. I see you even managed to bring in my luggage from the car. I appreciate that. Otherwise, I'd have to walk around your house without any clothes on."

She hoped he didn't notice the heated tint on her face at the thought of him parading through her house naked. "Well, I figured some things you can't possibly do without, and clothes are one of them."

And then she quickly left the room.

She looks cute when she blushes, Cole thought as he slipped into a pair of jeans and the shirt he'd taken out of his luggage. He glanced out the window and saw how hard the snow was still coming down and knew that chances were he'd be her houseguest tonight, regardless of how either of them felt about it. He didn't have a problem with it since a warm, cozy house was something he often craved, especially during those times as a ranger when he'd been forced to brave the elements during a stakeout.

But those days were long gone. His brother, Clint, had been the first to retire as a Texas Ranger last year, and then he had followed suit last month. With the money he'd made from selling Clint his share of the ranch his uncle had left to Clint, Casey and him, he'd made a number of lucrative business investments. Thanks to the expertise of his cousin, Spencer, the financial guru in the Westmoreland family, one investment in particular had paid off big-time. At the age of thirty-two Cole had been able to leave the Rangers a wealthy man.

He now had a stake in several business ventures, including the booming horse-breeding and -training business that his cousin, Durango, and his brother-in-law, McKinnon, had started a few years back. Clint had become a partner and after seeing the benefits of such an investment, Cole had recently become a partner, as well.

But he preferred being a silent partner, so he could be free to pursue other opportunities.

One such opportunity was a chance to purchase a helicopter business that provided taxi service between the various mountains to the people who lived on them. Besides that, he and his cousin Quade, who was taking early retirement from the secret service, had discussed the possibility of them joining forces to start a network of security companies. Clint had expressed an interest, too, as if he didn't have enough to do already with his involvement in training horses and taking on a wife.

Cole smiled when he thought of his confirmed-bachelor brother being a happily married man. Alyssa was just what Clint needed and Cole was happy for him, but knew that for himself, marriage was not anything he wanted anytime soon, if ever. He preferred being single and all the benefits it afforded. And now that he was no longer tied to a regular job, he had plenty of time to do whatever pleased him.

And getting to know Dr. Foreman pleased him. He made her nervous, he could tell. It wasn't intentional—the last thing he wanted was a skittish female around him. But he was attracted to her. That was a "gimme" and had been from the first. Hell, when she had picked up his hand to check his pulse, he'd almost come out of his skin. Her touch had sent all kinds of sensations through his body, and he'd been reminded of a need so hot and raw that he'd had to momentarily close his eyes against its intensity.

Up close he'd seen just how beautiful she was, more than he had even remembered. He had this full awareness of her. Back in Austin, he was a man known to appreciate beautiful women and he could definitely appreciate her. Every full-figured inch of her.

He knew she was attracted to him, too. There were the usual giveaways—the way her breathing changed when they were close, the way she studied his body when she thought he wasn't aware she was doing so, and then there was the way she would nervously moisten her lips. Lips he was dying to taste, sample and devour. To say he was fascinated with her, enamored by her, hot for her and had been from the first would be an understatement. The woman had the ability to steal his breath away without even trying.

And just as he knew the attraction was mutual, he could tell she was fighting it, probably because she assumed he was still a ranger. Durango had warned him that because of what had happened to her husband, she didn't date lawmen. But then he recalled Durango also saying she didn't date much at all.

Well, I'm going to have to be the one to change that, he decided as he sat at the small table with the tray of food in front of him. He glanced around the room. It had a nice, comfortable feel without looking feminine. The furniture was dark mahogany and the throw rugs scattered around on the floor were a nice touch. The bed was huge. It looked solid. Just the kind of bed you'd want to tangle with your woman on, between the sheets, on top of the covers, whatever suited your fancy.

In the distance he could hear the sound of pots and pans clinking as Patrina moved around in the kitchen. After taking the two painkillers she'd left, he tackled his stew. It was delicious. And she'd made him a huge sandwich. Man-size. Just like his desire for her.

When he finished the sandwich, Cole enjoyed the cake and coffee she'd also made. There was no doubt about it. The good doctor knew her way around a kitchen. His stomach was grateful.

The only thing he hated doing was eating alone, which was something he should be used to, since that was how he usually ate his meals. But it was hard knowing there was a pretty face he could look at in the other room.

"I came back to see if you needed anything else. Do you?"

He looked up at the sound of Patrina's voice. She was standing in the doorway. His gaze moved over her from head to toe, and he felt his blood pressure shoot to a level that had to be dangerous. She had a flawlessly beautiful face and a gorgeous body.

He took another sip of coffee while he continued to stare at her. Considering how much he was attracted to her, coupled with the fact that he hadn't slept with a woman in more than a year due to the number of undercover assignments he'd been involved in, what she'd asked was definitely a loaded question if ever he'd heard one.

He finally spoke. "Funny you should ask. Yes, there is something else I need."

Two

Patrina suddenly felt the weight of Cole's response on every inch of her shoulders. For some reason, she felt she needed to prepare for what he was about to say. Maybe she could tell from the way he was looking at her, with heated lust in his eyes. Or it could have possibly been the sudden shift in the air surrounding them, releasing something primal, something uninhibited, something better left capped, that warned her what could be coming. She just hoped he didn't say what she thought he was thinking.

Since Perry's death many men had attempted to date her—colleagues, friends of friends, guys Dale had introduced her to. None had succeeded. She preferred living an existence where she was not involved in a relationship, serious or otherwise, with any man. It was hard for some of her admirers to understand her position. They wouldn't take no for an answer. But none, she inwardly admitted, was as persistent as the man staring at her now.

She studied his expression and exhaled slowly. He'd made his statement and now it was time for her to ask what he meant by it. She walked farther into the room, paused by the table and asked her question. "And what else do you need, Cole?"

He didn't answer right away and she was aware that he was trying to decide if he really should. Good. Let him think about it. Some things were better left unsaid. She wasn't born yesterday and she had been a married woman at one time. She recognized the vibes, the tingle and the heat of lust. She knew enough about male testosterone and how it could get the best of a man sometimes. And she knew how not to become a victim when it got out of hand.

"I need company."

She blinked upon realizing that Cole had spoken. She studied his expression, searched his eyes. "Company?"

"Yes, company. I didn't like eating alone."

She had a sinking feeling that wasn't what he'd originally planned to say. She appreciated the fact that he had thought his answer through first. He didn't know her and there was a lot she didn't know about him. The only thing that was certain was the sexual chemistry between them. She was old enough and mature enough to recognize it for what it was worth. She was realistic enough to accept their attraction for what it was—wasted energy. The last thing she planned on doing was getting involved in an affair destined to go nowhere. She'd been married for five years to a wonderful man, was now a widow and wasn't interested in changing that status. Besides, Cole was a lawman, for heaven's sake.

"I told you why I didn't stay. I had things to do in the kitchen," she finally said, frowning and wondering if he was one of those self-absorbed men greedy for attention and looking for any willing female to give it to him.

"I want to get to know you better."

She saw the smile that touched his lips and the twinkle in his dark eyes. He was doing something to her, messing with her rational mind, while at the same time making breathing an effort for her. "Why?" she couldn't help asking.

He glanced out the window. "Because it looks like we're stuck in here together."

Patrina also fixed her gaze on the view outside the window. Snow was still falling, and according to the weather report on the radio, it wouldn't let up anytime soon. It would be this way for another couple of days. Whether she liked it or not, she was temporarily stranded with Cole Westmoreland.

She shook her head and quickly decided on a plan. "I think you should get back into bed and rest some. You're not out of the woods yet. I'm going to take this stuff to the kitchen and—"

"Promise." He met her gaze and she felt the lure in it. The automatic pull. "Promise you'll be back."

She knew she should fight it, resist it with everything she had. But then she felt she could handle it since she was used to men like Cole. She'd been raised with one and had spent a lot of her time watching him in action. Dale had been the consummate ladies' man. He'd used just about every charm he possessed, every pickup line in the book, to get girls. She glanced at the tray on the table. Good. Cole had taken the pain pills, which meant he would be getting drowsy in a little while. For the time being she would just humor him.

"Okay, I promise I'll be back."

She kept her promise and when she returned fifteen minutes later, he had gotten back into bed and…was wide awake. He evidently had more energy than she thought.

"I was beginning to wonder if you planned to return."

She took the wing chair across from the bed, folding her long skirt beneath her as she settled into it with a book in her hand. "I promised I would. I just wanted to catch the latest weather report on the radio," she said truthfully, although that wasn't the only thing that had detained her.

"And what did the report say?"

She sighed, not sure she wanted to tell him. "That we're in for a blizzard tonight and all day tomorrow."

He nodded. "Don't you ever get lonely living out here by yourself? Especially when the weather's like this?"

She shook her head. "No, because usually I stay overnight in town so I'll be available if my patients need me. It just so happens that I'm on vacation this week. I timed it so I would be taking time off when none of my patients were scheduled to deliver."

"And what happens if a baby decides to surprise its parents and arrive early?"

She laughed. "Trust me, it's happened before. But with this weather, they would just have to make their entrance into this world without me. There are other doctors on call when I'm not available."

"You delivered Durango and Savannah's baby."

She couldn't help the smile that touched her lips, remembering. "Yes, and that night I saw a side of Durango I thought I would never see."

"And what side was that?"

"The side that shows how much a man can actually love a woman and his child. I've known Durango for years, ever since I was a kid. Even before moving to Montana, he and his brothers and cousins used to visit your dad every summer on his mountain. Like McKinnon, my brother, Dale, was friends with all of them and none of us were surprised when Durango decided to come back to attend a university around here after finishing high school."

Cole nodded. He knew the story, having heard it a number of times. He couldn't help but admire a man like his father, Corey Westmoreland, who'd taken up so much time with his nephews. It hadn't been Corey's fault that Cole, Clint and Casey had grown up believing their father was dead. That was what their mother had told her triplets. Then on her deathbed a few years ago, she had confessed that their father was alive somewhere and hadn't died in a rodeo accident like they'd been told. The day after burying their mother, he and Clint had hired a private investigator to find their father. Casey hadn't been all that eager and had struggled hard with their mother's cover-up. He was glad to see how his sister and father had grown close over the past year. The reason Cole had come to town now was for the big party that Casey and his father's wife, Abby, were planning for Corey's birthday at the end of the month.

Cole glanced over at Patrina. There was one question he was dying to ask her. "Are you involved with someone, Patrina?"

He saw her guarded expression and knew his question was unexpected. She stared down at the book in her hand and without looking at him, she asked, "Why do you want to know?"

"Curious."

She lifted her head and met his gaze and immediately he felt it the moment their eyes connected. The sexual chemistry was so tangible there was no way it could be misinterpreted. It was more than a mere meeting of the minds. It was a meeting of something a whole lot more powerful, and while one part of him was embracing it as a challenge, another part was thinking he needed to step back and grab control, since no woman had affected him this way before. He studied her and saw her tiny frown. While he might see their mutual attraction as a challenge, he could tell she saw it as a nuisance.

An assured smile touched his lips when he repeated, "So, are you involved with anyone?"

"No."

"Do you want to become involved?" He decided to go ahead and ask her, curious about her answer. If it was yes, then that made things easy for him. But if she said no, then that meant a different game plan, since he definitely wanted her and was a man known to get what he wanted.

She leaned toward him and a part of him wished she hadn't. His mouth nearly dropped open when his gaze shifted from her face to the V of her blouse. When she'd leaned forward, he could see the tops of her firm, round breasts and the taut nipples that strained against the material of her blouse.

"Read my lips, Cole Westmoreland. I have no desire to become involved."

His gaze shifted from her breasts to her lips and he wanted to do something more than just read them. A fantasy suddenly flashed in his mind. Something he intended to file away for the day he did take possession of those lips that were now formed into a pout. To his way of thinking, a downright sexy pout.

He then moved his gaze from her lips up to her eyes. She had been watching him the entire time. He wanted her to know just how taken he was with her. He wanted her to know he was a man determined. But what he saw in her eyes alerted him to the fact that she was a woman just as determined. Where he planned on breaking down her resolve, her intentions were not to make it easy for him. In fact, there was no doubt she intended to make it downright difficult. There was no doubt a confrontation between them would be of the most sexually intense kind.

"And what if I were to tell you, Patrina Foreman, that I want to become involved with you?"

He watched something flash in the depths of her dark eyes as she pulled back. Anger. Fire. Heat. It could be all three, but it didn't bother him. He would eventually use them to his advantage. He'd never been fond of a woman who was too willing, anyway. A woman who didn't make things easy for him was the type he preferred and he couldn't recall when the last time was he'd encountered one such as that. One-night stands had become downright boring for him. In his last two sexual encounters, the women had been so eager they were the ones who'd asked him to take them to bed, claiming he wasn't moving fast enough to suit them.

"I would tell you that you were wasting your time. Take a good look at me, Cole. Do I look like a woman who could be easily swayed?"

Now that she'd given the invitation, he decided to take her up on her offer. He took a good look at her, not that he hadn't checked her out pretty much already. His gaze leisurely swept over her. She had a full figure, well endowed in all the right places, a real sexy and feminine body even in clothes. He didn't want to think how it would look out of clothes.

"Do I look like a woman who elicits uncontrollable lust in a man?"

Yes, he would say she did, but evidently she had other ideas. "What is the point you are trying to make?" he asked, deciding they needed to cut to the chase.

Her frown deepened as she stood up from the chair. "The point I'm trying to make is that I know your type. I'm sibling to one. You are man. I am woman. This thing, this attraction between us, is only a fluke. It's temporary. It's meaningless. For you it's just a whim. Men like you have them most of the time. It's an ingrained part of your nature. Women of all shapes and sizes flock to you. Throw themselves at your feet, plaster themselves across your bed, spread themselves for you to enjoy. And when it's all over, you wear a satisfied smirk on your face and walk away. In your mind you're thinking, next. And for you there is a next. And a next. I don't intend to be any man's *next*."

He considered her words—at least he tried to. It was hard when her breasts were heaving with every single word she spoke, every movement she made. And when she had placed her hands on her hips to glare at him, he had shifted his gaze from her breasts to her hips. Flaring, wide, absolutely plentiful. He could imagine himself…

"Women my size are a joke to men like you."

His head snapped up at that. "Excuse me?"

Her eyes narrowed. "You heard what I said. Men like you, cover-model potential, are drawn to women who are also cover-model potential. Granted, I might be your flavor of the moment, but don't think you can show up in town, bored with what you left behind in Texas and decide to sample the local treats while you are here in Montana."

Cole stared at her. Okay, she was partly right. While he had gotten bored with the easy lays and had thought it would be nice to find a woman interested in a couple of quickies while he was here visiting, he hadn't intentionally set his sights on her. That is, until he'd found himself in her house and in her bed. Opportunities weren't something he liked missing. He had to admit that he saw her as an opportunity to take care of an eleven-month sexual drought.

But the part she'd said about him being cover-model potential who would only be drawn to a woman who looked like a supermodel was so far from the truth it was a shame. He liked women. And when it came to them he didn't discriminate as to weight, size, creed or color. He liked them all. He appreciated them all. And if he had the energy he would try to please them all. Hell, he was single. He wasn't tied to anyone and didn't intend to be. He didn't take anything from a woman she didn't want to give, and most women let him know up front that they were in the giving mood.

Okay, it seemed Patrina wasn't in the giving mood. But there was a thing called seduction, and it was something he was pretty good at. Another thing he was good at was reading people, and he was focusing on reading what her lips weren't saying. She was so full of sensual emotions, such an abundance of sexual heat, it wasn't funny. Whether she recognized the signs or not, she was a woman who needed a roll in the hay as much as he did. He'd bet she hadn't engaged in any type of sexual activity since her husband died. Her reaction to him was a telltale sign. Although at the moment she was fighting it, specifically, fighting him, he didn't plan on letting her get away with it. In the end, she would thank him. Suddenly Cole felt an overpowering urge to prove his theories about her.

And Patrina, it seemed, had this farfetched notion that he wasn't really attracted to her. Maybe he ought to invite her to stick her hand under the bedcovers to see…and to feel just how attracted he was to her.

"Now, did I make myself clear?"

He stared at her for a long moment before replying, "Yes, you did. Now I think I need to make myself clear, as well."

She blinked. Then she frowned at him before saying. "All right. Go ahead."

Refusing to lie flat on his back any longer, he kicked the covers aside and eased out of bed. Surprised, she took a quick step back and he noticed how she tried averting her gaze from the crotch of his boxers. "I don't force myself on women, Patrina, so don't feel you aren't safe around me. But I do know that I can pick up the scent of a willing woman a mile away, and regardless of the fact that you're trying like hell to fight it, you *are* willing. Hell, you are so willing, certain parts of my body have shifted into ready mode just waiting for you to say the word. I won't force you, but at some point in time I'm going to give you just what you need or what you possibly don't know you need."

Her glare sharpened. "Oh, you see me as a sex-deprived widow, is that it?"

He considered her words and a slow smile touched his lips. "No, I don't see you that way, but before it's all over I will definitely make you a very merry widow. When I look at you I see a very sexy and desirable woman who—for whatever reason—has been denying herself the company of a man. Maybe it's because you're afraid to get close to another male after losing your husband, or it could be you're scared to let yourself go, uncomfortable with the thought of becoming a fulfilled woman in someone else's arms. I want to think that perhaps fate is the reason we ended up stranded here together, and only time will tell. But I will make you this promise. It won't be me who makes the first move. It won't be me who eventually asks us to share a bed. It will be you."

"When hell freezes over!"

His smile widened. "Take a look out the window, baby. To my way of thinking, it's getting there."

Patrina breathed out a long, frustrated sigh. She didn't know just what to make of Cole and she was trying real hard to control a temper she didn't know she had until now.

Where did he come off assuming she was open game? She had done a good deed by rescuing him from the storm and bringing him to her place to recover, not for him to pounce on her when he thought he had the first opportunity to do so. Okay, she would be the first to admit the vibes between them were strong. Stronger than she'd had with any man, but evidently they were sending out the wrong message. There was no doubt in her mind that a man who looked like him probably had women throwing themselves at him all the time; however, that was no reason for him to assume she wanted to be one of them. He thought he could turn her into a merry widow; the very thought was absurd. Besides, even if she was the least bit interested in him, which she wasn't, he would be the last person she'd want to become involved with. He was a Texas Ranger, a lawman, and she had decided the day she had buried Perry that she would not get involved with another lawman again.

"You have nothing else to say?" he asked.

Her lips twisted as she glared at him, trying to stay in control of her anger. "What do you expect me to say? We met last year briefly, but you assume you know me and everything about me. Someone must have told you that you're God's gift to women, a man who assumes every woman, regardless of shape, size or color, is looking for a romp between the sheets. You've been in my house less than eight hours and already you're making a play for me. Is this how you show your appreciation for my warm and caring hospitality?"

Cole frowned. If she thought she was going to turn the tables on him by making him feel guilty about anything, she was wrong. The bottom line was, he was man and she was woman. Neither of them was involved with anyone, and desire was flowing so thickly between them you could turn it into mortar to lay bricks. He wanted her, and whether she admitted it or not, she wanted him. Surely she couldn't fault him for finding her desirable, for wanting to take her to bed. Okay, he might have come on too strong, too quickly, but hell, she was the one looking at him with those hungry eyes when she thought he wasn't looking. He merely wanted her to know that when and if she decided to make a move, he was more than ready.

"Like I said, Patrina, I've never forced myself on a woman and I don't plan to start now. The last thing I want you to think is that I don't respect you, because I do. What's going on between us has nothing to do with respect. It's about the fulfillment of wants and needs. From what I've gathered, you've put yourself on a shelf and I'm at a loss as to why when you're so beautiful and desirable."

He leaned closer. "It's time you're taken off the shelf and I'm just the man who's bold enough to do it, and if that pisses you off, then so be it."

Her glare darkened. "How dare you!"

"How dare I what? How dare I be bold enough to remind you that you're a woman? Something you seem to want to forget? Well, look at me, Patrina, and what you'll see is a man who finds nothing wrong with noticing a woman as a woman and bringing it to that woman's attention if I have to."

Patrina tilted up her face, opened her mouth to tell him just what she thought of what he'd said when he suddenly leaned in even closer, and before she could draw in her next breath, he covered her mouth with his.

She thought of putting her strength into a shove to push him back, but the deep growl she heard from within his throat stopped her at the same time his tongue was eased into her mouth. What she hadn't expected were the sensations that tongue taking hold of hers evoked.

Anger quickly became curiosity, which immediately shifted to something she hadn't felt in so long she'd almost forgotten it existed—sexual hunger. And before she could stop it, it took control of her mind, body and senses. And as if that wasn't enough she felt one of his hands touch the center of her back to draw her closer into his heat.

His heat was as hot as anything she'd ever experienced, and he was sipping her up like he was obsessed with the taste of her. Willing her mind or body to resist him was not an option. Not when every fiber of her being was tuned in to his mouth and what he was doing to hers, so exquisitely poignant she wondered where he'd learned to kiss that way. He took, but at the same time he gave. There was no doubt that he was experienced when it came to the art of lovemaking. He was stirring to life within her sensations that were infusing every cell in her body, every nerve ending. The man was basically devouring her alive, and with a possessiveness she felt all the way to the bone.

And then it suddenly occurred to her that she was kissing him back. That hadn't been her initial plan, and then it quickly dawned on her that she really didn't have a plan. At the moment she was a willing participant who was handling Cole's assault on her mouth in the only way she knew how. Complete surrender.

Later she would rake herself over the coals for allowing him such liberties, for letting him turn her brain into mush, for making her feel things she hadn't felt in years. But for now, she wanted to savor, to relish and to enjoy the feel of being in a man's arms and being kissed by him this way. He was stoking a fire that had burned out long ago. And as she sank deeper into the strong arms that held her, she felt a flame being stirred from that fire, which only heightened her senses of him as a man.

Suddenly he pulled his mouth away and she watched as he clutched the bedpost as if what they'd shared was more than he'd bargained for, too. She took that opportunity to take a step back.

Cole drew in a deep breath. His head was spinning. His brain felt intoxicated and his body felt wildly alive. And all from a kiss. Whether Patrina admitted it or not, that kiss had served a very important purpose. It proved a number of things, but mainly that they were hot for each other. He opened his mouth to tell her just that, but she shoved an upraised finger in his face.

"Don't say it. Don't even think it," she warned. "It was just a kiss. It meant nothing."

He gave her a sharp look, zeroing in on lips that had just gotten thoroughly kissed. She wasn't being completely honest with herself or with him if she wanted to claim that the kiss had meant nothing when they both knew just the opposite. It *had* meant something.

"Think what you want, but I've proved a point," he said, deciding he'd had enough energy-draining activity for one day. Easing down on the bed, he ignored her glare as he slid back under the covers.

"And I've also done something else, as well," he said. Knowing he had her too mad to ask what that something else was, he then said, "I've initiated my plan to move you off that shelf. Although you're still there, you're no longer in the same spot. I've shifted you away from the side that's been cold for some time to a side better suited for you. And that, Patrina, is the hot side."

She stared at him like he'd totally lost his mind. But that was fine. She could think whatever she wanted, he thought as he closed his eyes. Like he'd said, he had proved a point, and besides, he had tasted her hot side.

And damned if he didn't like it. He liked it a hell of a lot.

Three

"Good morning."

Standing at the kitchen counter, Patrina paused, trying to get her thoughts and emotions under control before turning to face Cole. When she had awakened last night it was to discover she had fallen asleep in the chair next to the bed where he slept.

She had eased from the room to take a shower before climbing into her own bed and then had trouble sleeping, knowing he was in the room across the hall. Twice during the night she had gotten up to check on him and had seen he was still sleeping peacefully—and looking nothing like the man who was destined to turn her life upside down when awake.

She could vividly recall the first time she had seen him last year at Casey's party. The moment their gazes had connected she had felt something strong, so elemental, and it had shaken her to the core, nearly corrupted her nervous system and made her realize for the first time since Perry's death that she was capable of being attracted to another man. She had been totally confused by the intensity of that attraction and had been too taken aback by it to try to figure things out at the time.

Her intention had been to avoid Cole all evening that night at the party; however, that was something he would not let happen, and he'd finally cornered her and introduced himself. Like everyone else in these parts, she had heard about Corey's triplets, but other than Casey, she hadn't met them. Clint and Cole looked so much alike they could be identical, but there was something about Cole that stood out. Maybe it was his features, which were so compelling they'd taken her breath away the moment she'd seen him. Or it could have been the shape of his mouth—so intensely sexual it made you think of stolen kisses or had you not thinking at all. And then maybe, just maybe, it was the dark eyes that seemed capable of stripping you naked when they looked at you. Whatever it was, she had quickly reached the conclusion that like her brother, Cole was a ladies' man constantly on the prowl and she was a woman who refused to become his prey.

She had gotten the same impression about him when she'd seen him again six months later at Casey and McKinnon's wedding. The moment he had walked into the church and their gazes had connected, just like before, sexual chemistry, thick enough to almost smother you, had flowed between them all the way across the aisle of the church. Knowing she couldn't take the chance of him catching her at a vulnerable moment, she had left the church immediately after the wedding was over and skipped the reception, giving him no chance to exchange a single word with her.

Now, less than six months later he's a guest in her home.

Deciding it was time to acknowledge his presence, she plastered a smile on her face and turned around. "Good morning, Cole. H-how…"

Her words faltered as her gaze zeroed in on him standing there, casually lounging in the doorway that separated the kitchen from the dining room. He was shirtless and wearing a pair of jeans that rode low on his hips and looking sexier than any man had a right to be. And he was barefoot, which gave him an at-home look. A sprinkling of dark hair covered his muscular chest— and it was a chest so well defined she tried thinking of numerous reasons she should rub her hands across it.

It suddenly dawned on her that she was standing there staring at him, and just as she was raking her gaze over him, he was doing the same with her. She was wearing a pair of slacks and a pullover sweater and she didn't want to admit she had taken more time with her appearance than normal. The snow still hadn't let up outside, but she definitely felt heat on the inside.

"Something smells good."

His words were like a caress to her skin and she quickly turned back to the counter and leaned forward to reach down to get a frying pan out of the cabinet below, figuring she had ogled him long enough and any more was only asking for trouble. "I hope you're hungry," she said over her shoulder as she straightened.

"I am."

From the sound of his voice she could tell he'd moved into the room. In fact, he sounded as if he was right at her back. She was too nervous to turn around to see if that was the case.

"How do you like your eggs?" she asked.

"Um, I'm sure I'll enjoy them whatever way you prepare them."

It seemed he whispered the words right close to her ear. She swung around with the skillet in her hand only to have the front of her body hit smack up against his.

Before she could ask why he was standing so close, he reached out and took the skillet out of her hand. His lips curved into a smile. "Can't have you thinking of using this as a weapon," he said, placing it on the counter. He then leaned in closer. "I want to thank you for everything."

His mouth was almost touching hers and once she could release her gaze from his lips, she forced herself to wonder what exactly he was thanking her for. The kiss they had shared yesterday possibly? She doubted it since she figured his lips had kissed countless other women, and most, she was certain, had been more experienced in doing that sort of thing than she was. "What are you thanking me for?"

"For bringing me here, taking care of me and putting up with my straightforwardness about certain things."

Straightforwardness or arrogance? She quickly thought and knew just what *certain things* he was referring to. "I'm a doctor. I'm used to putting up with all kinds of people and their attitudes and dispositions."

"You're also a woman, Patrina," he said, looking her straight in the eye as he leaned in even closer. "And that's something I feel compelled to remind you of."

She noticed his gaze was lowering to her lips and a faint shiver ran down her spine. She could almost feel the heat radiating from him and licked her lips again. Instinct warned her to take a step back or be robbed of her concentration, but she couldn't since the counter was at her back.

It hit her then what his response to her had been. Why did he feel he should remind her of anything? The first time they had spent more than five minutes in each other's presence was yesterday. It wasn't like they really knew a lot about each other for him to decide on something like that. Stubbornness stiffened her spine. "You don't need to feel compelled to do anything, and basically you have no right. Besides, being a woman isn't anything I can forget."

He shrugged. "No, but it's something you evidently seem determined to ignore and I refused to let you do that. I want you to feel the passion."

She narrowed her gaze at the same time she opened her mouth to tell him that she had no intention of feeling anything when suddenly he swooped down and connected his mouth to hers. At first, everything inside her tensed, went on full alert, but then she relaxed and her mouth clung to his, and just like the day before, she automatically began kissing him back.

The hot fever she felt she had yesterday gripped her

in a way that had her wondering what she was doing and just what she was letting him do to her. She was actually melting under each stroke of his tongue and could feel the swell of her breasts pressed against his bare chest—that same chest she'd ogled just seconds earlier. Everything at that moment seemed so right, although in the back of her mind she knew it was all wrong. The texture of his mouth was manly, his flavor provocative, and the longer he kissed her, the more he was drawing her in, tempting her with a degree of desire she had forgotten could exist between a man and woman. This kiss was doing a mental breakdown of her senses in a way that had her moaning deep in her throat.

He was kissing her with a hunger she felt all the way to her toes and he refused to let up. Instead, he took her tongue in a relentless hold, as if savoring it, tangling with it, gave him immense pleasure. It was certainly giving her more pleasure than she had counted on. She'd never imagined something could be so intense until he'd kissed her last night, and this one was no different. If anything, it had even more fire.

Then suddenly his mouth softened on hers, just moments before he broke off the kiss. She let out a soft moan before automatically lowering her face onto his chest, not ready to look him in the eye while giving herself time to catch her breath. She ignored the warm feel of his hand gently caressing her back as if trying to soothe new life into her and wanted to protest that she was fine with her present life. She didn't want this—the passion, the awakening feelings that bordered on sensations she wasn't used to, sensations she had gotten over long ago. What she desperately needed was a chance to be alone, but since the weather was still ugly outside, she knew such a thing was next to impossible. Cole wasn't going anywhere and neither was she.

Cole was deep into his own thoughts as he continued to hold her, gently rubbing her back, while neither made an attempt at conversation. Just as well, since he figured the kiss—the second one they'd shared—had said enough. But then, it might not have. Patrina, he was discovering, was stubborn when it came to acknowledging some things. "I could have kept right on kissing you, you know," he said in a low voice, close to her ear. He figured she needed to know that.

He felt the faint tremor that touched her body, once, then again before she lifted her head and looked at him. The darkness of her eyes touched him in a way he found unnerving, and then with little or no control on his part, he lowered his head and gently brushed his lips across hers, feeling her shiver again in his arms.

"You're trying to be difficult," she accused breathlessly, while narrowing her gaze at him.

Her words, as well as her expression, brought a smile to his lips. She wasn't happy with him, but he was more than happy with her. He simply liked stoking her fire. "No, what I am is persistent," he corrected, drawing her closer. "I figure that sooner or later you'll come around to my way of thinking."

"Don't hold your breath."

Cole knew she really didn't have a clue about what she was doing to him. He felt his erection throb and quickly decided that maybe she did. There was no way she wasn't aware of how aroused he was. They were standing so close their bodies seemed to be plastered together. And for a moment he felt something, a fierce tightening in his gut, as well as a hard throb in his lower extremities that reminded him once again, and not too subtly, that he was a full-blooded male. And a hot one at that.

He was standing with his legs braced apart so that his thighs could snugly embrace hers and figured his aroused body part, which was unashamedly pressed against her center, made what was on his mind a dead giveaway. He tried dropping his gaze from hers and decided it wasn't a good idea when his eyes came to rest upon the necklace she wore around her neck. It was a gold heart and its resting place was right smack between her breasts. Nice plump breasts.

Feeling his gut tighten even more, he lifted his gaze and studied the look in her eyes, quickly reaching the conclusion that nothing had changed. The desire be-tween them was strong, intense as ever. But talk about someone being difficult, as far as he was concerned, she could be hailed as queen. He would, however, enjoy breaking down her resolve.

Deciding he had made his point for now, he released her from his arms and took a step back. "Do you need my help fixing breakfast?"

She tilted her head at an angle that showed the per-fection of her neck and the moistness of the lips he had kissed. "No, I don't need your help. You can sit in the living room and I'll call you when it's ready."

Cole chuckled as he crossed his arms over his chest. It was either that or he'd reach for her again and pull her into his arms and kiss her. "In other words, you want me out of the way."

"Yes, that's what I want."

"All right."

She eyed him like he'd given in too easy. "What?" he asked, smiling.

She lifted a brow and then, as if she didn't want to discuss anything with him any longer, she said, "Nothing. I'll call you when everything's ready." She then turned to the counter and presented her back to him.

He was tempted to reach out and brush her hair away from her neck and leave his mark there, but knew she wouldn't appreciate him doing something so outrageously bold. Hell, the back of her didn't look so bad, either. The denim of her jeans fit snugly over her shapely bottom. He forced his heart to beat at an even pace.

He smiled as he moved in the direction of her living room. Once there, he decided not to sit down as she had suggested. Instead, he glanced around, checked things out. The living room, like the other parts of the house, was nicely furnished and the furniture was solid and sturdy, the kind that was made to last and fit perfectly in this environment. Considering the weather in these parts, undoubtedly, it had to.

A thick, padded sofa and love seat made of rich leather looked inviting, and the throw rugs scattered about on the floor gave you the option of curling up in front of the fireplace. But one glance out the window brought forth a dreary picture. He often wondered how his father could endure the harshness of Montana's cold weather, high on his mountain, especially those days before Abby had returned to his life. But what of those times when he'd been up there alone, those harsh and cold winters when Corey Westmoreland had lived his life as a lonely man, pretty much the way Patrina was living hers—a lonely woman. A part of him wondered what right he had to make the assumption that her life was lonely. She had her work, which he figured she enjoyed, but still he felt she needed more. Like he'd always felt his mother had needed more.

He recalled as a little boy watching his beautiful mother deny herself the chance of falling in love again and living a happy life. Instead, she'd clung to the story she'd fabricated for her children and everyone else that her husband—the only man she could ever love—had died in a rodeo accident. Although Cole and his siblings had discovered later that Corey Westmoreland wasn't dead, in a way he was to Carolyn Roberts, since she had known she would never be the woman to have his heart.

Cole could recall a number of good men who'd come calling on his mother, trying to gain her interest, like his fourth-grade teacher, Mr. Jefferson. But none had been able to awaken the love she'd buried long before her triplets were born. She had died without the love or companionship of a good man. She had died in that same spot on the shelf where she'd placed herself for more than thirty years. And for a reason he didn't want to dwell on, he didn't want that for Patrina. Although he was not interested in a serious relationship with any woman, he had no problem being the one to initiate her return to a life filled with excitement, one filled with fun where she would want to take a part in all the things that went with it—such as sharing her bed with a man.

Cole moved in front of the fireplace and saw the framed photographs lined up on the mantel. His gaze went immediately to one in particular and knew he was seeing Patrina on her wedding day with the man who'd been her husband. From what he remembered Durango telling him, Patrina had been married five years before her husband was killed. After that she had thrown herself into her work. For some reason he couldn't help standing there staring at the photo for a long period of time.

According to Durango, Perry Foreman had been a good friend and a first-class lawman whose life had been shortened, taken away needlessly and way too soon, leaving a grieving wife behind. How long had it been? Over three years? He couldn't help wondering at what point the grieving stopped. When did a person decide to start living again?

He moved his gaze to another framed photograph. It was of Patrina with two other women. They were older women and he could see a strong family resemblance in their faces, notably the eyes and jaw. Her mother and grandmother, perhaps? He hadn't asked her about any living relatives. He knew about her brother, Dale, since they had met at Casey and McKinnon's wedding.

"I just put the biscuits in the oven. They won't take long to bake."

He turned at the sound of her voice. She was standing in the doorway that separated the kitchen from the living room and was about to turn back around when he said, "Wait a second. Who are these two women in this photo with you?"

He watched as her mouth curved in a smile, and its vibrancy almost dulled his senses. This was probably the first genuine smile she'd given him. "That's my mother and grandmother," she said, coming into the room and standing what he guessed she figured was a safe distance from him.

"Are they still living?"

He saw the sadness that crept into her eyes. "No, both are gone. I miss them." Then a slight smile touched her lips. "Everybody misses them. They were the town's midwives and so was my great-grandmother. That's four generations of Epperson women delivering babies around these parts. I don't know of many people born on the outskirts of town who weren't delivered by them. Although they trained me to follow in their footsteps, I decided to go to medical school to offer my patients the best of both worlds."

He nodded. "Dale is all the family you have?"

She chuckled and the rich sound carried through the room. "Yes, and trust me when I say that he's enough."

From the tone of her voice he could tell she shared a close relationship with her brother, the same kind he shared with Casey and Clint.

"I take it this is your husband in the other photo."

She didn't say anything for a moment, just stared at the photo. "Yes," she finally said. "That's me and Perry on our wedding day. He was a good man."

"So I heard. Durango and McKinnon liked him."

She put her hands in the pockets of her jeans and

leaned against the corner of the fireplace. "Everybody liked Perry. He was that kind of person, real easy to like. And he was a good sheriff." She was quiet for a short while before adding, "He should not have gotten killed that night."

"But he did," he decided to remind her, not that he was insensitive to the pain he heard in her voice, pain she hadn't let go of even after three years. But he was thinking more along the lines of the life she was now denying herself. He didn't understand why he felt the need to push the issue every chance he got, but he did.

"You don't have to remind me of that, Cole." She straightened her stance and all but snapped, "And Perry dying is one of the reasons I will never become involved with a lawman again."

His brows rose, not in surprise since that was something else Durango had shared with him, but because of the determination he heard in her words. As far as she was concerned her mind was made up, pretty well set on the matter. "Why?" he decided to ask, wanting to hear her reason from her own lips. "Because he died in the line of duty?"

"Yes. It was a senseless death and as far as I'm concerned that reason is good enough."

Before he could say anything to that she walked back into the kitchen. He hated telling her, but that reason wasn't good enough. She refused to believe that men who entered the world of fighting crime do so knowing their lives could be taken away at any time, but the chance of doing good, even for a short while, outweighed the risk of becoming a casualty. He had enjoyed his life as a Texas Ranger and although he knew the good guys didn't always win, they did make a difference. The only reason he and Clint were no longer rangers had nothing to do with the risks involved with the job, but had everything to do with taking advantage of other opportunities that had come their way.

"Everything is ready now, Cole."

The sound of her voice touched him in a purely elemental way. It was intensely feminine and he liked hearing it. "I'll be there in a minute," he called back to her.

As he began walking toward the bedroom to put on a shirt, he figured any other man would respect her wishes and let her live whatever kind of life she wanted, but he wasn't just any other man. He was a man very much attracted to her. He was a man of action and not someone who did anything on an idle whim. And at the moment, it seemed that he was the one who was able to push her buttons. The two times they had kissed, he had tasted her passion and her hunger, had almost drowned in it. She had enjoyed kissing him as much as he had enjoyed kissing her. There was no mistake about that. Letting her remain on that shelf was not an option. She was a woman who was meant to give and receive pleasure and he intended to do everything in his power to convince her of that.

Four

Patrina was conscious of Cole the moment he entered the kitchen. She didn't look up from placing the food items on the table; instead, her thoughts dwelled on the last time she'd shared breakfast in this house with a man who wasn't Dale. It definitely had been a long time.

She heard the water running and knew he was at the sink washing his hands. "Everything looks good, Patrina."

Knowing he was so close at hand was making it impossible for her to relax. The man had more or less stated that he planned to seduce her, or would at least try. She bet he figured that two kisses in less than twenty-four hours wasn't bad. She was determined he wouldn't make it to number three. "Thanks, Cole. Everything is ready."

"Aren't you going to join me?"

He had come to stand close beside her and his nearness almost startled her. She hadn't heard him move. "I'd love to have some company," he added.

She looked up. His jeans still hung low on his hips, but at least he had put on a shirt. She was grateful for that. She then met his gaze. "I have things to do."

"You have to eat sometime." And then he moved slightly closer and asked, "Why do I get the distinct impression that you're afraid of me? Or is it that you're afraid of what I do to you? What we do to each other?"

She looked at him. At his facial features that were so intensely handsome they made her ache, at his eyes so impressively sexy they sent a shiver racing through her. She wanted to feel irritation, but felt a throb of desire instead. She breathed in deeply, fighting the impulse to do something really foolish like accept things as they were between them and go ahead and savor the moment. She held back. A part of her was fighting to draw the line, especially with him, although she was finding it harder and harder to do so.

"Tell me. Why are you so persistent about that?" she demanded softly.

"Because of this," he said in a voice just as soft, while reaching out and taking her hand in his. "Feel it. Feel the passion."

The moment they touched, she gasped, and although she tried valiantly to fight it, she felt currents of electricity dart up her spine. Warm sensations began flooding her insides while goose bumps formed on her arm. Her stomach began tightening, and her nervous system seemed to be on overload. She met his gaze, became locked into it and saw hot desire in the dark depths of his eyes.

She blinked, hoping she was mistaken by what she saw. It was the same look he'd given her from the first. The longer his gaze held hers, the more convinced she was that she was not mistaken.

He smoothly withdrew his hand from hers, dropped it to his side before saying, "I think I've made my point."

Whether he made it or not, it was a point not too well taken. One she intended to ignore. "Think whatever you want, Cole. I suggest you sit down and eat before your food gets cold."

"Ladies first."

She regarded him steadily as she took the chair that he held out for her. "Thanks."

His mouth curved into a sexy smile. "You're more than welcome."

It was then that she realized she had done exactly what he'd wanted by sitting down to eat with him. He sat across from her and followed her lead and said grace. Then he began helping himself to everything. There was plenty of food. She'd served biscuits, sausages, eggs, bacon, orange juice and coffee. One thing she'd quickly found out about him was that he enjoyed eating.

He took a sip of coffee. "You make the best coffee. Hot, strong, not too sweet. Just right."

She didn't want to say that's how Perry had liked his coffee. She had an instinctive feeling he wouldn't appreciate hearing it.

"Your television works, right?"

She glanced up and looked across the table at him. "Yes."

"Why don't you have it on?"

She shrugged before biting into a piece of bacon. "I usually don't have time to watch television. Not nowadays, anyway. I'm too busy with the work I do at the hospital and the clinic. Besides, there's nothing on most of the time other than those reality shows or cop shows. I can do without either."

"You mean you're not a *CSI* fan?" he asked, smiling, before taking another sip of his coffee.

"I don't want to have anything to do with anything connected to law enforcement and that includes watching it on television."

"I'm sure your position on that hasn't made your local police department happy."

She placed her fork beside her plate and glared at him. "Don't try twisting my words. I'm not saying that I don't support or appreciate what they do. I was a lawman's wife too long not to. All I'm saying is that it's a life I don't want to be a part of ever again."

Cole didn't say anything but couldn't help wondering if her words, like the ones she had spoken earlier, were meant to deter him since she assumed he was still a Texas Ranger. No one in his family, not even his father and sister, knew he had left the agency. He planned to surprise them with the news when he saw them at his father's birthday party. Of course Clint knew, and because they were working on a business deal together, his cousin Quade was aware of it.

He had seen no reason not to mention it to Patrina—

until now. With what she had just said and the statement she'd made earlier, he felt the need to prove to her that what he did for a living didn't matter when it came to the passion sizzling between them. One had nothing to do with the other.

"You're free to watch anything on television you like, Cole. I'm into a good book, anyway."

He glanced over at her. "A Rock Mason novel?"

She smiled as she leaned back in her chair. "Yes, a Rock Mason novel."

He couldn't help but smile since they both knew that Rock Mason was actually his cousin, Stone Westmoreland. Stone's wife, Madison, had given birth to a son a couple of months ago. "Have you figured out who's going to be the next victim yet?" he couldn't help asking her. Stone was an ace when it came to writing thrillers.

"No, not yet. The book's definitely a page-turner, though. Stone has another bestseller under his belt."

They didn't say anything else for a while as they continued to eat. At one point Patrina risked glancing across the table at Cole to find him sipping his coffee and staring at her. She quickly refocused on her food.

"Is there anything you need me to do, Patrina?"

She quickly glanced up and met his gaze. "Anything like what?"

He shrugged. "Chop wood for the fireplace, help wash the breakfast dishes, go outside and play in the snow…you name it and I'm all for it."

The thought of the last item made her chuckle. She couldn't see the two of them doing something as outrageous as playing outside in the snow. "There's already enough wood chopped. Dale took care of that when he was passing through last month. As far as the dishes are concerned, I plan to just rinse them off and place them in the dishwasher."

"And the offer for us to go outside and play in the snow?" he asked, still staring at her.

"I'll pass on that one. It's too cold outside."

"You of all people should be used to it," Cole said, chuckling. "Come outside with me. I dare you."

She shook her head. "Don't waste your time daring me because I'm not going outside. Besides, you still need to take it easy."

"I feel fine," he assured her. Without breaking their gazes he pushed his chair away from the table and stood. "Why don't you go get comfortable and start on your book while I load up the dishwasher?"

"Cole, you don't have to do that."

"But I want to. I need something to keep me busy. Go ahead and start reading your book."

"I started reading it last night."

He nodded as he began gathering the dishes off the table. "I know. I woke up a few times and saw you sitting in the chair reading. Then I saw you'd fallen asleep with the book in your hand. The last time I woke up and glanced over at the chair, it was empty."

Patrina gave a small, dismissive shrug. "The chair was getting uncomfortable and I needed to get into bed."

He paused for a moment and looked over and met her gaze. "You could have shared mine. I would not have minded and would gladly have moved over and made room for you." He resumed collecting the dishes.

She let out a deep sigh. "You don't plan on letting up, do you."

He didn't bother looking at her when he said, "I've already explained the situation to you, Patrina. Nothing has changed. In fact, I'm more determined than ever." He walked over to the sink and began placing the dishes in it.

"Why?"

With that one question, one word, he turned around, and she was amazed at how intensely she could feel the direct hit of his gaze. "We covered that already," he said, speaking in a calm and rational tone. "You already know why. But if you need reminding, the simple fact is, I want you and you want me."

"And what if I said I *don't* want you? That I don't have any sexual interest in you whatsoever?" she said, getting to her feet and glaring across the room at him.

"Then I'd say you were lying or that you're a woman who doesn't know what she wants."

Patrina took offense. "Nothing is going to happen between us, Cole," she said, determined to stand her ground.

"You want to bet?" he challenged. "You felt the same thing I did when I touched your hand earlier. And it was there in the kisses we've shared. Deny it all you want, sweetheart, but even now I can feel your heat. I can almost taste it. And eventually, I *will* taste it," he said.

"You think I'm a woman who can't resist your charms?"

He crossed his arms over his chest and leaned back against the counter. His gaze roved over her from head to toe before he said, "No, but I do admit to being a man who can't seem to resist yours."

Thinking that he apparently liked having the last word, and seeing no reason to continue a conversation with him that was going nowhere, Patrina walked out of the kitchen. Once in the living room she forced herself to breathe in deeply. Of all the arrogant men she'd ever encountered, Cole Westmoreland took the cake.

And the nerve of him to claim that he was a man who couldn't resist her charms. Yeah, right. Did he actually expect her to believe that? Suddenly a tightness tugged deep in her stomach. What if he was telling the truth? What if the desire they felt for each other was just that strong? Just that powerful? What if it became uncontrollable?

She quickly did a mental review of everything that had happened since she'd brought him into her home, especially that time while, when folding up clothes, she'd looked up to find him staring at her. Could two people actually connect that spontaneously? Could they suddenly want each other to a degree where they would lose their minds, as well as their common sense, to passion?

She was definitely out of her element here. She and Perry had been childhood sweethearts, had known each other since junior high school when his family had moved into the area. There had never been a rushed moment in their relationship. He was easygoing and patient. The fact that they'd made love for the first time on their wedding night attested to that. All those years when they had dated, they had managed to control their overzealous hormones with very little effort. With Perry she had never felt pressured or overwhelmed. And she'd certainly never felt the intense sexual chemistry she felt with Cole. But still...

Just because they were attracted to each other was no reason to act on that attraction. Of course Cole saw things differently and was of the belief their attraction alone was enough reason to act on it. He was clearly a man who had no qualms about indulging in a casual relationship and expected her to follow suit. Well, she had news for him. There wasn't that much passion in the world that would make her consider such a thing.

Leaving the living room, she went into her bedroom and in a bout of both anger and frustration, she slammed the door shut behind her. She crossed the room and snatched the book off the dresser. *Fine!* Let him spend some time alone since he only saw her as a body he was eager to pounce on. Maybe if she ignored him, that would eventually knock some sense into him.

Stretching out on the bed, she opened her book and began reading. She refused to let Cole get on her last nerve.

He'd have to be an idiot not to know he'd made Patrina mad again, Cole thought, as he loaded the last plate into the dishwasher. And if she thought ignoring him would do the trick, she was sadly mistaken. She had to come out of hiding sooner or later. He had enough to keep himself busy until she did. He loved working word puzzles and had a ton of them packed in his luggage. There was nothing like stimulating his mind, since thanks to Patrina the rest of him was already there.

Feeling frustration settling in, he walked over to the window and stared out at the still-falling snow. But despite its thickness, in the distance he could see the mountains, snow-covered and definitely a beautiful sight, postcard perfect.

Deciding he would forgo watching television and start on those word puzzles, he walked out of the living room toward the guest room. He paused a moment by Patrina's closed bedroom door, tempted to knock. But then he decided he was in enough hot water with her already. It was time to chill and allow her time to come to terms with everything he'd said to her. Besides, she couldn't stay locked up behind closed doors all day.

A smile touched his lips when he thought of a way to eventually get her out of there. She had to come out and eat some time.

Patrina glanced over at the clock and then stretched out on the bed to change positions. It was late afternoon already and a glance out the window showed it was snowing more heavily than before.

She couldn't believe she had been reading nearly nonstop since the morning, but at least it had given her time by herself. The last thing she'd wanted was another encounter with Cole. There was no doubt in her mind that he had his mind set on wearing down her defenses, and she intended to resist him every step of the way.

Suddenly she sat up in bed and sniffed the air. A delicious aroma was coming from the kitchen. She got out of bed and opened the door and found the scent was even stronger. Curious, she walked out into the hall and headed for the kitchen. Once there she paused in the doorway. Cole was standing beside the stove stirring a pot, and even with a huge spoon in his hand and an apron tied around his waist, she was fully aware of his potent masculinity.

"What are you doing?" she couldn't help asking.

He glanced over at her and smiled. She tried not to notice what that smile did to her insides. She breathed in to stop her stomach from doing flips. "I thought I'd be the one to prepare dinner tonight," he said, giving her a thorough once-over, and making it obvious he was doing so.

She tried ignoring him. "I didn't know you could cook."

He chuckled. "There's a lot you don't know about me, but yes, I can cook and I like doing it. By the time the table is set everything will be ready. I thought I'd try some of my Texas chili on you."

She leaned against the counter. "It smells good."

"Thanks, and later you'll agree that it tastes as good as it smells."

She rolled her eyes. The man was so overly confident it was a shame. "What do you need me to do?"

"Nothing. I have everything taken care of. The rolls are about ready to come out of the oven and the salad is in the refrigerator. Did you enjoy your rest?"

A part of her felt guilty knowing that while she'd been stretched across the bed reading, he had been busy at work in the kitchen. "Yes, but you should have let me help you."

He chuckled as he took the rolls out of the oven. "No way. I got the distinct impression this morning that you'd had enough of me for a while and needed your space."

He had certainly read things correctly, she thought, moving to the sink to wash her hands. "The least I can do is help by setting the table."

Not waiting for him to say whether she could help or not, she went to the cabinets to take down the plates. After all, it was *her* kitchen.

"Did you finish your book?"

She glanced at him over her shoulder and became far too aware of his stance. He was no longer standing in front of the stove, but had moved to lean a hip against the counter. She was totally conscious of the sexy way his jeans fit his body, and it made her suddenly feel warm. Then there was the way his shirt stretched across a muscular chest and the way—

"Well, did you?"

She blinked upon realizing he was asking her something. The deep baritone of his voice vibrated along every nerve in her body. "Did I what?"

He smiled in a way that was just as sexy as his stance. "Did you finish the book?"

"Not yet. But things are getting pretty interesting," she said quietly, thinking it wasn't just happening that way in the book. She met his dark gaze and felt shivers go up her spine.

"Are you going to set the table?"

Patrina looked down and then it hit her that she was standing there holding the plates in her hands and staring. "Yes, I'm going to do it," she said, pushing away from the cabinet. He moved at the same time she did and the next thing she knew they were facing each other. He took the plates out of her hands and placed them on the table.

He then gave her his complete attention. "I know you needed your space, but I didn't like it," he said huskily.

She didn't know what to say, so she just stood there and stared up at him, finding it hard not to do so. In fact, she was finding it hard to concentrate on anything at the moment—except the perfect specimen of a man standing in front of her.

"Why didn't you like it?" she heard herself asking, and nervously licked her lips. She couldn't help noticing how his gaze latched on to the movement of her tongue.

"Because I would have preferred you spend time with me," he said in a barely audible voice.

Although she already had an idea, she asked, anyway. "Doing what?"

His sexy smile became sexier when he said, "Word puzzles."

She blinked again, not sure she'd heard him correctly. "Word puzzles?"

He nodded slowly. "Yes, I'm good at working them."

As far as she was concerned, that wasn't the only thing he was good at working. He was definitely doing a good job working her. Her body was tingling from the mere fact that he was standing so close. It wouldn't take much to reach up and loop her arms around his neck, and then pull his mouth down to hers and then…

"Don't think it, Patrina. Just do it," he whispered throatily, leaning in closer.

Their gazes locked and she wondered how he'd known what she'd been thinking. It must have shown in her eyes, or it could have been the sound of her breathing. She couldn't help noticing it had gotten rather choppy.

"You're hesitating. Let me go ahead and get you started," he whispered in a raspy voice before reaching out and cupping her face in his hands, And at the same time he shifted his body, specifically his hips, to press against hers, aligning their bodies perfectly.

Whenever he touched her, her body would automatically respond and it didn't behave any differently now. But she couldn't explain the degree with which it was doing so. Desire was rushing through her with a force that nearly left her breathless and the nipples of her breasts were feeling taut, tender, sensitive. Heat flared low in her body, making it hard to think, so she was doing what he had asked her to do several times. She was feeling the passion.

She could feel the heat of his gaze as his mouth inched closer to her lips; she could feel the hard evidence of his desire that was pressed against her abdomen. And she could also feel the touch of his hand on her face, warm, strong and steady.

Then their lips touched and she no longer felt the passion, she tasted it. It had a flavor all its own. Tart, tingly and so incredibly arousing it had her heart pounding relentlessly in her chest as he continued to kiss her with a single-minded purpose that went deeper than anything she'd ever felt before. It was a primal need she didn't know she was capable of.

And then she noticed his hands were no longer on her

face but had moved to her rear end. He was pressing her closer to him, letting her feel the state of his arousal. Instinctively she moved her hips against it and he took the kiss deeper.

Not bothering to question why, she gave in to her needs, needs he was forcing her to admit she had. His tongue aggressively dueled with hers and she wrapped her arms around his neck to lock their mouths in place. With her firm grip the only thing he was capable of doing was changing the angle of the kiss and in doing so, she heard him groan deep in his throat.

One of them, she thought, had on too many clothes and quickly concluded it had to be him. She felt his hard erection pressed against her, and now she wanted to really feel it, to touch it, take it in her hand and hold it. As if her hands had a mind of their own, they moved from around his neck and reached down and began pulling out his shirt before lowering his zipper and then reaching for his belt buckle with an urgency she couldn't control.

And then the buzzer on the stove went off.

For her it had the effect of ice water being tossed on a hot surface, and she pulled away from him with such speed that she almost tripped in the process. He reached out to keep her from falling, but she jerked away and turned her back to him. But not before she saw that his shirt had been pulled out of his pants and that his zipper was down. Embarrassment flooded her face in knowing she had done both and had intended to go even further.

"Patrina?"

She refused to turn around to let him look at her. A

part of her wished that somehow the floor would open up and swallow her whole. How in the world had she let things get so out of hand?

"Patrina, turn around and look at me."

"No," she said over her shoulder as she began moving toward the living room. "I don't want to look at you. I want to be left alone."

"What you are, Patrina, is afraid," he said, and from the sound of it, he was right on her heels, but she refused to slow down to see if he was or not. "You are afraid that you might give in to your passion, continue to feel it and be driven to admit to the very thing you're trying so hard to deny."

That did it. She suddenly stopped and turned and he all but ran into her and made her lose her balance. She tumbled onto the sofa and he went with her, and when her back hit the leather cushion, he ended up sprawled on top of her, his face just inches from hers.

She opened her mouth to scream at him to get off her, but no words formed in her throat. Instead, her gaze latched on to a pair of sensual lips that were so close to hers she could feel his heated breath. When she shifted her gaze, she also saw vibrant fire lighting the dark depths of his eyes. Looking into them seemed to have a hypnotic effect and she felt her entire body getting hot all over.

He didn't say anything. He continued to look at her with the same intensity as she was looking at him, and she found herself wondering why she'd never shared something of this degree, something of this level of intimacy with Perry. There had been plenty of physical contact between them and she had enjoyed their kisses, but they hadn't been full of fire like the ones Cole delivered. In analyzing things now, it seemed that she and Perry were too close as friends to become so intimate as lovers. He had to be the kindest and gentlest man she'd ever known and those characteristics extended into their bedroom. When they had made love it seemed like he'd been intent on keeping their level of intimacy at a minimum. It was as if he'd thought of her as a piece of crystal, something meant to be handled carefully or else it would break.

Cole wasn't treating her like a piece of crystal. He was treating her like a woman he thought could deliver passion to match his. Personally she thought he was expecting way too much from her. But then he had a way of making her body tingle just by being near her. And a part of her believed that he couldn't give any woman just a minimum level of intimacy. A man of his sensual nature was only capable of delivering a level that would go way beyond the max. It would be off the charts. The thought of that made her breath catch in her throat.

She noted he was still staring at her. She also noted his lips were moving closer. Then they paused as if they refused to move any farther. And she became aware of what he was doing. He was leaving the decision to take things beyond what they were right now to her. He wouldn't push her any further.

The look in his eyes made sensations stir within her, made her blood flow through her veins in a way that just couldn't be normal. They were lying on the sofa fully clothed, yet she could still feel his heat. Not only was she feeling it, she seemed to be absorbing it, right through her clothes and into her skin.

She could no longer question what he was doing to her or why. She wasn't dealing with a mild-mannered man like Perry. At the moment there wasn't a single thing refined about Cole that she could think of. He was a man who went after what he wanted without any finesse or skilled diplomacy.

They didn't say anything for a long moment. They continued to lie together and stare at each other, fueling the fire between them, a fire destined to become an inferno. She felt the full length of him, every muscle of his perfect physique, pressed against her, and she began to fall deeper and deeper into a sea of sexual desire. Then she heard herself give a little moan before looping her arms around his neck to bring his mouth down to hers.

The moment their lips touched, his tongue entered her mouth like it had every right to do so, and like those other times, it took over not only her mouth but her senses. He was kissing her with pure, unadulterated possession. And as if she'd been given her cue, she kissed him back with a fervor she didn't know she had until meeting him.

Moments later, and she wasn't sure just how much later, he broke off the kiss and pressed his forehead against hers as if to catch his breath. She needed to catch her breath, also. And then as if he couldn't help himself, he shifted their bodies sideways and then leaned forward and placed a brief, erotic kiss on her lips that caused a stirring in her stomach, an urgency that seemed to consume her.

For a long moment they lay there in silence while he held her, then both got to their feet. A slow smile curved his mouth. "I think we should go into the kitchen and eat now," he said in a warmly seductive voice as he pulled her closer into his arms.

"And then," he added while holding her gaze with an intensity that made her shudder, "what takes place after dinner will be strictly your call."

Five

Cole glanced across the table at Patrina. She hadn't said much since they had begun eating. He figured what he'd told her moments ago in the living room had given her something to think about.

She was stubborn, filled with more spirit and fire than any woman he'd ever met. Considering those things, she probably would still not admit to wanting him, and definitely would not act on it, although they had kissed about four times now. And they hadn't been chaste kisses, either, but the kind that set your body on fire. Hell, his body was still burning and he was hard as a rock.

At least if nothing else he was proving to her that she was indeed a sensual woman, something else she still probably wanted to deny. All and all, he felt that when it came to Patrina Foreman, he still had one hell of a challenge on his hands. The good doctor just refused to acknowledge what was so blatantly obvious. She needed a good roll in the hay just as much as he did. He refused to let up trying to convince her that indulging in a couple of sexual encounters with him was just what she needed.

Deciding the silence between them had lasted long enough, he figured it was time to get her talking. She was very dedicated to her job, so he decided to begin there. He leaned back in his chair, took a sip of his wine and asked, "What exactly do you do at that clinic, Patrina?"

It took her a while but she finally lifted her head and looked at him. And then she was frowning. "Why do you want to know?"

He shrugged. "Because I'm interested."

She gave a doubtful snort, which meant she didn't believe him. He understood what she was doing. For a little while she had let her guard down with him and now she was trying to recover ground and put it back up. "And why would you be interested?"

He had an answer for her. "Because I'm interested in anything that involves you," he said, completely honest and totally unfazed by the cold look she was giving him.

It was hard to believe that less than an hour ago she had been warm and willing in his arms. She'd kissed him with as much passion as he'd been kissing her. The memory of their tumble onto the couch and the way their lips had locked still had heat thrumming through him. He was in worse shape now than before mainly because he had gotten a good taste of that bottled-up passion and was determined to get her off that damn shelf now more than ever.

"So tell me," he said when she refused to start talking. "I'm really interested in what you do at that clinic, so tell me."

"What if I don't want to?" she asked through tight lips.

He smiled. "Um, I can think of several ways to make you talk."

Evidently the ones he'd been thinking of crossed her mind, too, and she quickly dropped her gaze and began studying her glass of wine. Then she said, "It's a women's clinic that provides free services, which include physicals, breasts exams, pap smears, pregnancy testing, comprehensive health education, as well as many other types of needed services."

"How often are you there?"

She shrugged. "It's voluntary and I'm there as much as I can be, usually at least a few hours each day. I wish I could do more. Funding is tight and the medical equipment we need isn't cheap. We depend on private donations to ensure ongoing services for women who lack access to adequate health care."

"Pregnant women?"

"*All* women. Last year, our outreach program provided services to over a thousand homeless women. We believe all women deserve excellent health care, regardless of their ability to pay, and…"

Cole listened as she continued talking and could tell that her work at the clinic was something she was very passionate about. But then, he had discovered that she was a very passionate person…and very expressive. He couldn't stop looking at her while she was speaking and how she used her hands to get several points across. She had nice hands and he would do just about anything to feel those hands on him. She'd come close, had even unzipped his pants before that damn timer on the stove had gone off. Hell, he wished he'd remembered to turn the thing off when he'd taken the rolls out the oven.

His gaze moved from her hands over her face, scanning her eyebrows, cheekbone and nose before latching on to her lips. Damn, they were kissable lips and he wouldn't mind tasting them again. But what he really wanted was her naked and in bed with him. He wanted to move in place between her lush thighs and get inside her, move in and out, see the expression on her face when he made her come. Feel the shuddering power of his release when he did likewise.

"Sorry…" She paused and drew in a quick breath. "I didn't mean to go on and on like that. I kind of get carried away."

Her words pulled him back in. "No reason to apologize," he quickly said. "I found everything you said interesting." *At least I did when I wasn't thinking about making love to you.*

"Since you cooked, the least I can do is take care of the dishes," she said, getting to her feet.

He could tell she was nervous about what she perceived as his expectations on how the evening should end. When she reached for his plate, he grabbed hold of her hand and gently gripped her fingers with his. "I don't like it when you seem afraid of me, Patrina." He felt the shiver that passed through her and then that same shiver passed through him.

She tried pulling her hand free but he kept a tight hold and wouldn't let it go. "I'm not afraid of you, Cole. I'm just unsure about a lot of things right now."

"Don't be unsure of anything," he said quietly. "Especially when it involves us."

He watched as she drew a deep breath and then released it before saying, "But there is no *us,* Cole."

He regarded her for several silent seconds, saw the determined glint in her gaze, the stubborn set of her jaw. "You didn't think that a couple of hours ago on that sofa. Need I remind you of what almost happened?"

She tugged her hand from his and narrowed her eyes. "It was a mistake."

The corners of his mouth curved into a smile. "It was more like satisfaction to me. I could have kept on kissing you and you could have kept on kissing me." He was tempted to go ahead and tell her, anyway, in blatant, plain English of the most erotic kind just where all that kissing could have led, but he decided not to. The fiery spark in her eyes was a clear indication that she wouldn't appreciate hearing it. She wasn't too happy with him right now, which meant they were back to square one.

"Look, Patrina, if it makes you happy, I'll help you do the dishes and then we can go to bed." At her piercing glare he quickly said, "Separate beds, of course. This has been a long and tiring day for me." And that, he thought, was putting it mildly. Spending another night with a hard-on was something he wasn't looking forward to. "But then, if you want to share my bed I have nothing against it," he said in a low voice that sounded like a sexual rumble even to his own ears.

"I'm sleeping in my bed tonight and you're sleeping in yours," she said, as if saying it to him would make it happen.

"If that's the way you want things."

"It is."

"Then at least let me help you with the dishes," he said, taking another sip of his wine, resisting the urge to reach out to take her hand in his again, tumble her into his lap, pour some of the wine down the front of her blouse and be so bold as to lap the wine up with his tongue.

"I can handle the dishes on my own," she said, breaking into his thoughts while stacking up the plates. "I don't need your help."

He stood and slid his hands into the pockets of his jeans, thinking she had to be the most stubborn woman he had encountered in a long time. "Fine, I'll leave you to it, then."

She regarded him carefully, as if she didn't believe for one minute he would give in to her that easily. When she saw that he was, she said, "Good."

He moved away from the table, but before he walked out of the kitchen he turned to her. "No, what would be good in my book—actually better than good—is sharing a bed with you."

Patrina released a deep, frustrated sigh of relief the moment she heard the shower going in the guest room. That relief was short-lived when her mind was suddenly filled with visions of a naked Cole standing under a spray of water.

She closed her eyes, fighting off the forbidden

thoughts, refusing to let her mind go there, but it seemed to be going there, anyway. She couldn't forget how they had tumbled onto the sofa, how his solid, muscled body had been on top of hers, how his firm thighs had worked themselves between her legs in such a way that denim rubbing again denim had been an actual turn-on.

It didn't do much for her to remember how she had latched on to his mouth to finish what had started in the kitchen. Once again he had reminded her just how much of a female she was. Just how much passion she had been missing out on—both before and after Perry's death.

She quickly opened her eyes, not wanting to go there, refusing to think about it. Perry had been simply great in the bedroom; he'd just handled her a lot differently than Cole would—if given the chance. But she refused to give him the chance and the sooner he realized that, the better off the both of them would be.

She and Cole were playing this vicious game of tug-of-war where he was determined to come out the winner. And she was just as determined that he be the loser. Considering the kitchen scene earlier when she had come close to touching him in an intimate way, as well as the tumble onto the sofa, she would go so far as to admit that for a little while, she had gotten caught up in passion and had allowed him to break down her defenses. But she had recovered, was of sound mind, on top of her game, and simply refused to let him get an advantage again. She had to show him that she wasn't just some naive country girl.

She wasn't born yesterday and was well aware that it was all about sex to him. Nothing more than a quick tumble between the sheets. But then, knowing Cole, she suspected there would be nothing quick about it. He would draw it out, savor every second. He would strive to make her experience things that she had never experienced before, even during her five years of marriage. Already his kisses had taken her into unfamiliar territory.

Okay, she would be the first to admit that curiosity and desire had almost gotten the best of her, had almost done her in, but she was back in control. Talking about the clinic had helped. It had made her remember just how many women she'd counseled about the importance of being accountable for their actions and whatever decisions they made. It was time for her to take a dose of her own medicine.

It didn't take her long to finish the dishes and sweep the floor, deciding to have both done before Cole took a notion to return. She would retire early tonight and finish reading her book. But first she wanted to listen to the weather report. She needed to know just how much longer it would be before Cole was able to leave so she could get her life back to how it had been before he arrived—all work and no play, filled with apathy, definitely lacking passion. Before he had set foot in her house, the only desire she had was for the work she did at the doctor's office she owned and at the clinic. She would admit she lived a boring life. *Would it really be totally wrong, absolutely insane to sample some of what Cole was offering, and for once to forget about everything and everyone other than myself and my own needs?*

He said he wanted her and she had no reason not to believe him, especially once it appeared he had been aroused all day, at least whenever he was in her presence. She was a medical doctor, so she recognized the obvious signs. But then, she was a woman, as well, and given that, she had done more than noted the signs. For a while she had gotten caught up in it, gloried in the fact that he found her so desirable he couldn't control his body's reaction.

The thought that she could do something like that to a man, especially a man like Cole, was totally mind-boggling. Maybe she should rethink her position, give in to her desires, to see where it got the both of them. It wasn't like he was a permanent resident of Bozeman, so chances were that when the weather cleared for him to leave, she probably wouldn't be seeing him again while he was visiting Casey. She knew about the huge party Casey and Abby had planned for Corey later in the month, and she had every intention of attending. Even if she and Cole did share a bed before he left, by the time the party happened, she should be able to put the affair behind her so that when she saw him again, she wouldn't have a flare-up of passion, at least not of the degree she was having now. So maybe sleeping with him—to work him out of her system—wasn't such a bad idea.

Deciding she'd drunk too much wine at dinner for her to be considering such a thing, she moved across the kitchen to turn on the radio, as well as to put on a pot of coffee. She needed to sober up her brain cells.

Not much later she was standing at the window looking out with a cup of coffee in her hand. It was dark outside and still snowing. According to the weather report, things should start clearing up by late tomorrow evening or early the following day. That meant that this could be the last night Cole would have to stay under her roof. There was a chance he could leave for Casey and McKinnon's place before dark tomorrow. Then she could have her house all to herself again. She wouldn't have to worry about dressing decently if she didn't want to, or having a man underfoot. Nor would she have to worry about her hormones going wacky on her from a purely male dimpled smile or a dark lustful gaze.

"Is it still snowing?"

She quickly turned, sloshing some of the hot coffee on her hand. "Ouch."

Before she knew what was happening, Cole had quickly crossed the room to take the cup out of her hand and place it on the counter. "What are you trying to do? Burn yourself?" he asked in a deep voice filled with concern.

"You startled me," she accused.

"Sorry. I didn't mean to."

She tried ignoring the sensual huskiness in his voice. "Well, you did."

It was then that she noticed what he was wearing. In her opinion it was very little. He was barefoot with only a pair of boxer pajama bottoms, similar to the ones Dale liked to wear, but she never had reason to notice how snug they fit Dale. They were a silk pair and she was sure they belonged to a set. So where was the top part? Or at the very least, a matching robe.

Maybe she should at least be grateful that he was wearing anything at all, since some men preferred sleeping in the nude. But then, this wasn't his house. It was hers and under those circumstances he didn't have a choice in the matter.

But still...even with the boxer shorts there were a few things she couldn't help but notice. Like the fact he was still aroused. The cut of the boxers made that much completely obvious. She didn't want to stare but she found that she couldn't help herself. He was huge and as packed as any man had a right to be and then some. She subconsciously clamped her inner thighs together at the thought of something that size going into her. There was no way she wouldn't get stretched to the limit.

"So what do you think?"

She blinked and quickly shifted her gaze to his face. "About what?"

"The weather," he said, his dark gaze holding hers.

She couldn't help wondering if they were really discussing the weather. Regardless, she intended to play right along. "It's my understanding it should start clearing up tomorrow."

There was a bit of silence, then he said, "That means I'll be able to leave."

"Yes. I'm sure Casey will be glad to see you."

"Just like I'm sure you'll be glad to be all alone again."

Patrina suddenly felt a shiver of apprehension run up her spine. Would she really be glad to be all alone again?

"There's a full moon in the sky," he said quietly.

It was then that she noticed he was no longer looking at her but was looking out the window and up at the sky. She pondered his comment and wondered if it had any specific meaning. When she couldn't think of one she said, "And?" She figured there had to be more.

Although he didn't look at her, she saw his smile. "According to Ian, each full moon has a different meaning and a magical purpose," he said as he continued to gaze out the window and look at the sky.

Ian was Cole's cousin and considered the astronomer in the Westmoreland family because he had a degree in physics and had once worked for NASA. Ian was now the owner of a beautiful casino on Lake Tahoe. "And what do you think is the meaning of this full moon?" she couldn't help but ask.

He turned to her. "A full moon in April is the Seed Moon. It's the time to plant your seeds of desire in Mother Earth."

She raised a suspicious brow. "And you distinctly remember Ian saying that?"

His smile widened as he turned back to the window. "No. He gave me a book and I distinctly recall reading it."

"Oh." *Planting seeds of desire in Mother Earth.* She wasn't about to ask how that was done. But she couldn't deny it had her thinking, making a number of possibilities flow through her mind. Planting seeds of desire sounded a lot like setting someone up for seduction.

"Like I told you yesterday," Cole began, breaking into her thoughts, "neither Casey nor my father was expecting me this soon and they don't have any idea what day I arrived, so if you prefer, I won't let them know I spent some time here, stranded during the snowstorm with you."

"Why should it matter?" she asked. "Nothing happened between us."

He looked at her, raised an arched brow. "Nothing?"

She shrugged. "Okay, we kissed a few times."

"Yes, we did, didn't we?" he said softly, his gaze latched on to her lips. His dark eyes then shifted and held hers and she began to feel a sharp ache below her stomach.

"Yes," she finally answered. "We did."

"Want to do it again?"

That was one question she hadn't expected, yet she should not have been surprised that he had asked it. In the past thirty hours, she had discovered that Cole Westmoreland was a man who did or said whatever pleased him.

She opened her mouth to say that, no, she didn't want to do it again, then immediately closed it, thinking who was she kidding? She enjoyed kissing him and, yes, she wanted to do it again since it probably would be the last time she did so. He would be leaving tomorrow and chances were their paths wouldn't cross again—at least not in such an intimate setting.

She glanced out the window, thinking that the most sensible thing to do was turn and escape to her bedroom and not have any more contact with him. But for some reason she didn't want to think sensibly. She really didn't want to think at all, and the only time she couldn't think was when she was in his arms sharing a kiss.

"Patrina?"

She returned her gaze to his. "Perhaps," she said softly.

He arched a brow. "Perhaps?"

She nodded. "Perhaps, I want to do it again."

He gave her a level look. "Don't you know for certain?"

Patrina heard the slight tremor in his voice. "Well, maybe I prefer that you take your time and convince me that I do."

Her words seemed to hang between them as they stared

at each other, and for some reason, all she could think about was his mouth making her pulse race. And then he broke into her thoughts when he said in a gentle yet throaty voice, "I hope you understand what you're asking."

Oh, I understand all right, but it'll only be limited to kissing. She could handle that. Her throat suddenly felt tight, constricted, but she managed to force through enough sound to say, "I understand what I'm asking, Cole."

As soon as she stated her affirmation, she was pulled into strong, muscular arms.

Six

The first thing Cole wanted to do was taste her. He couldn't resist. Just one quick taste and then he would go about his business, taking his time to convince her that they needed to kiss again and again—definitely a lot longer each and every time.

His mouth brushed hers, just long enough to snake out his tongue and caress her bottom lip with its tip. He heard her sharp intake of breath and quickly pulled back on her moan. He did it again, a second longer this time, a little more provocatively when he wiggled the tip of his tongue while caressing the tantalizing surface of her upper lip.

He withdrew when she released another moan, this one throatier than the last and saw that her eyes had closed and her lips were moist from where his tongue had been. He liked the look of it. He also liked the look in her eyes when she reopened them to stare at him. He saw something hot and sensuous in their depths and fought for control not to say the hell with it and pull her into his arms and give her a long, hungry kiss.

Deciding to take the degree of her desire, as well as his, to another level, one that he could sufficiently handle, he reached out and with the tip of his finger, traced a path from her moist bottom lip down past her jaw to where her pulse was beating wildly in her throat. She said nothing while watching him attentively, but he could hear the unevenness of her breathing.

And then his lips and tongue replaced his finger while they moved all over her face, wanting to leave his mark everywhere on her features. And when he felt a shiver pass through her, he knew she was ready for something heavier and pulled her closer into his arms and greedily claimed her mouth in a long, slow kiss that made shivers run through her body even more than before.

Moments later, he pulled back and whispered the question close to her moist lips. "Want to try another one?"

Instead of answering, she nodded, and then he was back at her lips, devouring them in a way that shook him to the core. Never had his tongue been so ravenous for a woman's mouth; never had his palate been so famished. He could go on kissing her all night, but he wanted each one to be slow, long and fulfilling. And from the sound of her moans, they were.

He thought that this type of seduction suited her perfectly. Something slow and detailed while stirring her passion. With each stroke of his tongue he was able to discover just what she liked, what she had never experienced before and just what she wanted him to do again.

He also discovered what part of her mouth gave her the most pleasure, what part of it his tongue touched that made her moan the loudest, made her desire the strongest. He knew he could make her come just from kissing her if he were to turn up the heat a notch, and a part of him was pushed to do just that. That would lead into him giving her another type of kiss while at the same time experiencing a different taste of her.

The thought of doing so made his body harden even more, made his erection throb in a way that had him clutching for breath. All she'd given him was the liberty to kiss her. However, he intended to show her that when it came to kissing, there was no such thing as limitations. Kissing came in several forms and it could be done to a number of places, not confined just to the lips. No parts of the body were exempt. When she'd affirmed her understanding, he doubted that she knew the full extent of where it could lead. But he, on the other hand, understood perfectly and intended to take whatever kisses he delivered to the highest level possible.

He eased down on the windowsill, found it sturdy enough to hold his weight and pulled her to stand between his open legs, which put him eye to eye with her chest. He drew in a tight breath when he noticed how the nipples of her breasts were straining against her blouse as if begging to be freed. And he had no qualms about obliging the pair.

Still holding Patrina's gaze he began undoing the buttons, and each one exposed more of her black lacy bra. When all the buttons were undone, he eased the blouse from her arms and shoulders.

"You're only supposed to kiss me," he heard her remind him in a ragged voice.

"I know and I shall," he said throatily, letting his fingers move to the front clasp of her bra. "But kissing comes in many forms."

Then with a flick of his fingers her bra opened and her breasts burst forth. His mouth and hand were on them immediately, lightly cupping one while his mouth greedily devoured the other. He knew the moment she lifted her arms and held his head to her breasts, evidently thinking if she didn't do so he would stop. But there was no way he could stop. The taste of her was being absorbed into everything about him that was male, and her luscious essence—hot and enticing—was playing havoc with his senses.

She moaned his name over and over, and the more he heard it, the more he wanted to make her say it that much more, with even more meaning. He decided to put his other hand, the one that was free at the moment, to work and knew just where he wanted it to be and what he wanted it to do.

Reaching down he found the snap to her slacks and slowly worked it free to open it. She was so wrapped up in what he was doing to her breasts that she was unaware of what he was doing to the lower part of her body. He tugged her pants apart at the waist and the moment he did so, he inserted his hand inside and his fingers inched past the flimsy material of her panties to cup her feminine mound. He felt her body go still at the intimate touch and he freed the nipple in his mouth long enough to glance up and meet her gaze.

"Wh-what are you doing?" she asked in a strained voice, but she didn't pull away.

He chose his words carefully and spoke softly. "Like I said earlier, kissing comes in several forms. Will you trust me tonight to introduce you to a few of them?"

She said nothing as her gaze held his and he knew she was trying to come to terms with what he was saying, trying to decide just what she should do. He realized in asking her to trust him that he was asking a lot of her when she had no idea what he intended to do. And at that moment, he couldn't help wondering what was going on in that pretty little head of hers.

Patrina stood there and stared down at Cole, specifically at his mouth, which had been suckling at her breasts. She recalled how earlier those same lips and tongue had driven her crazy with desire, had her body still tingling. And now he wanted to use his mouth on her again, in other places, and she had an idea where.

During the five years of their marriage, she and Perry had never engaged in what she knew Cole was hinting at, and she couldn't help the sensations that flooded her stomach at the thought of participating in such an intimate act with him. To say she'd never been curious about it would be a lie, and now Cole was offering her the chance to indulge. Should she take it?

As if sensing that she was on the borderline, his fingers slowly began to move and the heated core of her began throbbing at the intimate contact. He was stroking new life into that part of her, creating a need she'd never known she had.

Her gaze shifted from his mouth to his eyes, which were boring into hers with an intensity that almost took her breath away. "Tell me," he whispered softly. "Tell me I can kiss you here," he said, and at the same time he inserted a single finger inside her to let her know just where he meant.

She sucked in a deep breath, suddenly feeling exposed, vulnerable and filled with a fire, the degree of which she hadn't known was possible for her. And it was taking over her senses, literally burning them to a cinder and making her act the part of someone she really didn't know. She could only close her eyes against such intense desire.

"Patrina."

She opened her eyes to meet his intense gaze and the look she saw there took her breath away. He wanted her. He *really* wanted her. Probably just as much as she wanted him. He wanted to introduce her to something new and different and she knew that she wanted the same thing.

"Yes," she whispered softly. "You can kiss me there."

She saw the smile that touched his lips and he didn't waste any time pulling her slacks down past her knees and taking her panties right along with them, leaving her feminine mound fully exposed for his private viewing. She closed her eyes but knew the exact moment he dropped to his knees in front of her and felt the strong hands that gently parted her thighs. She fought to remain standing when she felt him bury the bridge of his nose in the curls covering her mound, and she fought to retain her ability to breathe the moment he inserted his tongue inside her.

And like a meal he just had to devour, he tightened his hold on her thighs to keep her steady while his mouth went to work on her, the tip of his tongue piercing her with desire so strong and deep she cried out from something so totally unexpected, as well as something so profoundly intense.

She opened her eyes for a heated second and looked down only to see his head buried between her legs. Each and every stroke of his tongue was precision quick, lightning sharp, and was sending her over the edge in a way she'd never gone before.

She bit her lip in an effort not to cry out again, but cried out, anyway. She felt her knees buckling beneath her, but the firm grip of his hands on her thighs kept her standing. She grasped the sides of his head, telling herself she needed to pull him away, but instead, found she was placing pressure to keep him right there. He was exploring the insides of her body, the areas where his tongue could reach, and she was too overcome with passion to stop him. In fact, she heard her whispers of "Don't stop" over and over again.

Then suddenly, she felt her entire body filled with electrified sensations that ripped through her with a force that had her screaming his name, and she couldn't do anything but ride the incredible waves that were carrying her to some unknown destination. Frissons of pleasure attacked every cell of her body before she shook with the force of an orgasm the likes of which she'd never experienced before.

And just when she thought she couldn't possibly take

any more, couldn't stand on her feet a second longer, she suddenly felt herself scooped into strong arms.

"Wait, I'm too heavy."

"No, you're not," he said, gathering her up.

She buried her face in the warm, muscular texture of his chest and felt them moving. She wasn't sure where he was taking her and at the moment she didn't care.

But when she felt the softness of the mattress against her back, she knew. She opened her eyes and watched as he went about removing her shoes and socks and tossing them aside before tugging her jeans and panties completely off.

He gazed down at her naked body with heated desire before leaning over and kissing her lips in a slow, thorough exchange. Moments later he drew back from the kiss and in a surprise move pulled the covers over her, then tucked her in tenderly, as if seeing to her comfort. He then leaned over and kissed her again, and this time when he withdrew, he held her gaze and whispered, "Good night, Patrina. Sleep well."

She felt too weak to respond, so she said nothing. She lay there and watched as he crossed the room to the door, opened it and eased out, gently closing it behind him.

The moment Cole stepped into the hall he leaned against the nearest wall and drew in a sharp breath. It had taken all the control he could muster not to crawl into bed with Patrina, especially when her eyes had looked so inviting. Never had he wanted a woman more, and with his history, that said a lot.

There was something about her that brought out his

primal instincts, instincts that he always thought he could control. But with her he couldn't. It was as if after their first kiss he had become nearly obsessed with kissing her every chance he got, consumed with the taste of her and wanting to discover and explore all the different facets of that taste.

Tonight he had.

He had tasted her lips, her breasts and the very essence of her femininity, everything that made her the beautiful and desirable woman she was. If he had lingered in that bedroom with her a minute longer, he would have been tempted to strip off his boxers and join her in bed to find the heaven he knew awaited him between her lush thighs. She stirred a need within him that even now had him weak in the knees.

He lifted his hand to touch his mouth and couldn't help but smile. There was no way his mouth and tongue hadn't gotten addicted to her taste. Everything about her was perfect—the shape of her breasts, the flare of her thighs, the shape of her mouth, lips—everything.

Knowing if he didn't move well away from her bedroom door he would be tempted to go back into the room, he forced himself to walk toward the kitchen, needing some of the coffee she had made earlier.

A few moments later he was standing back at the window gazing out and holding a cup of coffee in his hand. What he'd told Patrina earlier about the full moon was true. He'd always had an interest in astronomy himself, but had never taken the time to develop that interest and had been surprised when he'd discovered he had a cousin who had.

He couldn't help but smile when he thought about his eleven male cousins and how he and Clint had been able to bond with them in a way that made it seem they had known each other all their lives and not just a few years. Quade had been the first one they had met, and only because he had shown up in Austin wanting to know why they were having his uncle investigated, and had been more than mildly surprised when they'd told him that the uncle he knew was their biological father—a father who didn't know they existed. Durango and Stone had been next, since they'd been in Montana when he and Clint had arrived to meet Corey.

He then thought about what he'd told Patrina earlier about not letting anyone know he'd been stranded here with her. He knew how some small towns operated. Patrina was a highly respected doctor and he wouldn't do anything to tarnish that. Although she was a widow, old enough to do whatever she wanted, some wouldn't see it that way. Besides, what they did was nobody's business but theirs.

Moving away from the window, Cole walked over to the counter to pour another cup of coffee. Although he wished otherwise, he was too keyed up to sleep. A cold shower would probably do him justice. Just the thought that Patrina would be sleeping in the room across the hall from him gave him a sexual ache that wouldn't go away, an erection that refused to go down.

For as long as he lived, he would never forget the look on her face when her orgasm had struck. It had been simply priceless and one he would love seeing again. The intensity of it had him wondering if she'd ever had one of that magnitude before.

He turned when he heard a sound and looked up to find Patrina standing in the doorway. Her hair was flowing around her shoulders and her features glowed with that womanly look—the one he enjoyed seeing on her. She was wearing a beautiful blue silk robe and the way it was draped around her curves showed what a shapely body she had. It was his opinion that she looked sexy as hell.

"I couldn't sleep," she said softly, her eyes locked with his.

He crossed the room to come to a stop directly in front of her, being careful not to get too close. He would definitely lose control if he touched her. Just inhaling her scent was doing a number on him already. "Would you like a cup of coffee?" he heard himself asking.

He watched as she shook her head. "No, coffee isn't what I need."

He drew in a tight breath, almost too afraid to ask, but knew he had to do so, anyway. "What is it that you need?"

The dark eyes that gazed back at him were filled with an expression she wasn't trying to hide, a sexual allure he could actually feel all the way to the bone. A fierce abundance of desire rammed through him when she responded in a soft and sexy voice, "You. I need you, Cole."

Seven

Patrina stood and watched Cole as he stood staring at her. She wondered what he was thinking and was certain he'd heard what she said. Saying it hadn't been easy, probably a few of the hardest words she'd ever spoken. But she had lain in bed, totally satisfied and remembering what he'd done to her right here in the kitchen, first while sitting on the windowledge and then on his knees. She wanted more. She *needed* more.

He'd always told her to feel the passion, but tonight he had taken those feelings to another level, and thanks to him she had done more than just felt the passion. She had experienced it in a way she never had before. That was in no way taking anything from Perry. It was just giving Cole his due. He was experienced when it came to pleasing women; he had a skill you didn't have to wonder how it had been acquired. The man was totally awesome and had a mouth that was undeniably lethal.

"Do you fully understand what you're saying?"

He'd asked her a similar question earlier tonight in this kitchen when he had wanted to kiss her. At the time she had said she understood because she'd been more than certain that she had. It hadn't taken long to discover that she hadn't understood the full extent of anything.

She definitely hadn't understood or known the degree of her passion. But Cole had. Somehow he had sensed it, had homed in on it from the first and immediately set out to taste it.

And tonight he'd gotten more than a taste. He'd gotten a huge whopping sample. But so had she. While he had taken control of her body, soul and mind, she had been driven to a need of gigantic proportion. And just to think she hadn't indulged in the full scope of what was possible. And more than anything she wanted to. Tomorrow he would be leaving and that would be it. The finale. But a part of her didn't want their time together to end.

"Yes, I fully understand," she finally said while holding his gaze and hoping he saw what was in her eyes—her determination, her heartfelt desire and now…her impatience.

She moved, took a step closer to him at the same time that he came forward, and suddenly she was in his arms. The fire they had ignited earlier was now a blaze and when he captured her mouth in his, the only thing she could think of was that this was where she belonged.

No man had ever possessed her this way. His hands seemed to be everywhere, all over her. The robe was stripped from her body, leaving her completely naked, but things didn't stop there. It seemed they were just beginning. He backed her out of the kitchen into the living room. Once there he stripped out of his boxers and the size of his erection had her blinking to make sure her eyes weren't playing tricks on her. He was huge. She should not have been surprised, but seeing him in the flesh was sending shivers down her body.

"You sure about this?"

She glanced up at him. Even now, with them standing facing each other as naked as two people could be, he was giving her a chance to change her mind.

Seeing the size of him was enough reason to consider doing so. But she wanted this. She needed this and she had to assure him. "Yes, I'm sure about this as long as you realize I don't come close to the level of experience or expertise that you're probably used to."

Cole nodded. A smile touched his lips. "I'm glad you don't."

And then he was pulling her into his arms, and when flesh melded into flesh, he kissed her with a longing she felt all the way to her toes. Her mouth opened fully to his, as far as it could stretch, and their tongues entwined, mingled, and their breathing combined, enticing her to feel things she could only experience with him. And then she found herself swept into strong arms. But the kissing continued. In fact, he picked up the pace, going deeper, making it hotter and more urgent.

He lifted his head and his gaze burned down into hers. It took her several seconds to catch her breath…as well as realize they were moving and that Cole was walking with her in his arms from the living room toward the bedroom he'd occupied for the past two days.

When they reached their destination he placed her on her feet beside the bed and she knew once again he was making sure this was what she wanted. She would have to get into his bed on her own accord. She looked at the neatly made bed, a representation of his handiwork, and marveled at how tidy a job he'd done. It was nothing like the haphazard-looking made-up beds she was used to whenever Dale came to visit.

Knowing he was watching her intently, she took a step closer to the bed and turned down the covers, and without saying anything she slid between the sheets and then looked at him expectantly. She felt totally aroused to see him standing there, naked with a huge erection and a tantalizing smile tugging at the corners of his mouth.

She was no longer angry with herself for being weak where Cole was concerned. Instead, she had accepted the fact that she was a woman with needs—needs she had tried ignoring for more than three years. And they would be needs she would once again ignore once Cole left. What she was taking with him was some *me* time. For once she would think of no one but herself and do something that would make her happy and satisfied.

"We're sleeping in tomorrow," Cole said in a voice so sexy it made her breath lock in her throat, and she scooted over when he joined her in the bed. It was queen-size, and a good fit for the two of them. The size of the bed vanished from her mind the moment he shifted and pulled her into his arms, claiming her lips in the process.

The kiss was everything she had gotten used to, had come to expect. His tongue was driving her crazy, stirring up her passion and sending shivers all through her body. It was the same body that his hands were all over, becoming reacquainted with all her intimate places. He was making it obvious that his focus was on pleasing her. She was touched by the gesture and decided to follow his lead. However, her focus would be on pleasing him.

She felt one of his hands slide between her legs, touching what she now considered her hot spot. His fingers began exploring at will, familiar territory to them now. She felt an instinctive need to touch him, as well, and slightly shifting her body, she reached down and took him into her hands. He released her mouth to pull in a sharp breath the moment he felt her touch.

He felt hard and smooth both at the same time, warm to the touch, huge in her hand. Then she began moving her hand, stroking him with an ease that surprised her. She became fascinated by what she was doing, totally enthralled with the way her fingers glided softly back and forth across the silken tip. And when she glanced up at Cole and met his gaze, what she saw in the dark depths took her breath away, made her aware of just how affected he was by her intimate touch.

Without saying anything he lowered his head and that same mouth he had used just moments earlier on hers now targeted her breasts. He drew between his lips an aroused peak and began sucking on it in a way that made her cry out his name.

She pulled her hand off him when he shifted their positions to place himself over her and used his knee to farther nudge her legs apart. He gazed down at her, giving her one last chance to stop him from going further. Instead she took the hand that had stroked him earlier and skimmed his chin and whispered, "I want this, Cole. I want you."

On a deep guttural groan he entered her and her body automatically arched, then proceeded to stretch to accommodate him. She felt all her inner muscles grab hold of him, begin clenching him as every nerve between her legs became sensitive to the invasion. She inhaled the masculine scent of him, the musky scent of sex, when he began moving, with quick, even strokes that sent her nearly over the edge with each hard thrust.

And then when she thought she couldn't possibly take any more, felt her body almost splintering in two, he gave one last hard thrust that triggered his release at the same time her body shattered into a thousand pieces. Too late it hit her that they had forgotten something, but there was nothing they could do about it now. Tremors were rocking her body to the core, and the only thing that registered on her mind was how he was making her feel at this very moment. And when he leaned down, enveloped her more deeply in his arms and captured her mouth with his, she felt herself tumbling once again into a sea of desire.

Cole came awake, not sure how long he'd been asleep. He glanced at the woman securely tucked in his arms and licked his lips. His mouth still tasted of her, her scent was all over his skin, just as he was certain his scent was all over hers. He recalled the exact moment she had come apart, triggering his body to do likewise. It had been one hell of a joining. Filled with fire, passion... He thought further, closing his eyes when realization hit—one that had been unprotected.

He let out a frustrated moan. How could he have been so careless? Condoms were tucked away in his wallet. It wasn't like he didn't have any. He just hadn't thought of using one. It would be the first time he'd ever made love with a woman without protection.

He again glanced at Patrina. She was sleeping with a satisfied look on her face. And rightly so. Their joining had been nothing short of magnificent. It had left them so drained they'd drifted off to sleep in each others' arms.

They had to talk and it was a discussion that couldn't wait until morning. She needed to know what he hadn't done—or more precisely what he might have carelessly done. He hated rousing her from sleep but leaned over close to her ear and whispered, "Patrina."

He said her name several times before she finally forced her eyes open to look at him. Before he could fix his mouth to say anything, she reached up and looped her arms around his neck, and on a soft groan she pulled his mouth down to hers.

Sensations skyrocketed through him and he returned her kiss with a passion that went all the way to the bone and instinctively, once again, he moved and positioned his body over hers. And when her thighs parted for him, he pressed down, entered her, filling her completely. And then their bodies began mating once again and every time he surged forward into her aroused flesh, he felt his own body trembling, blatant testimony to his own ardent desire.

And when she wrapped her legs tightly around him, as if to hold him inside, he was filled with a sense of possession that until now had been foreign to him. He ached for her and would always ache for her. And she would be the only one who could satisfy that ache, as she was doing now.

And when her body began quivering uncontrollably just moments before she released his mouth to scream his name, he knew her power over him was undeniable and absolute. Just like he'd known he would, he helplessly followed her over the edge and into the grips of an orgasm so mind-blowingly strong that he felt his every nerve ending leap to life. He also knew she had become an addiction that would be hard as hell for him to kick.

"It's stopped snowing."

Cole's statement filtered through Patrina's mind as she glanced out the window. Not only had it stopped snowing, but a semblance of sun was forcing its way through the Montana clouds. She couldn't say anything because she knew what that meant. He would be leaving.

As if he read her thoughts, he said, "I plan on being here for a while, Patrina. I need to call the car-rental agency and let them know about the car so they can go get it and bring me another one here."

He pulled her deeper into his arms and then said, "And I meant what I said yesterday. None of my family knew I was coming this early, so they aren't going to be worried and wondering where I am. I want my being here with you these past two days to be our secret."

She knew he wanted that to protect her reputation and she appreciated it, but it wasn't necessary. She opened her mouth to tell him so, but then he kissed her and she could no longer think. She could only feel.

After they had made love that first time, they had fallen asleep and had awakened to make love again, and again, into the wee hours of the morning. If she never made love to another man again, she would be satisfied. But then, she couldn't imagine ever being in another man's arms this way, sharing his bed. In the space of forty-eight hours she had gone from being tucked away safely on a shelf to having been brought down and placed on a counter where she had experienced things she never thought could happen between a man and woman.

Cole released her mouth and said in a strained voice, "I didn't use protection, Patrina. Not that first time or any of the other times. I'm sorry for being so careless. That's not the way I operate. If anything develops from it, I will take full responsibility. You and my child won't want for anything."

She met his gaze, was touched by what he said but felt that this, too, wasn't necessary, although she wished she could say the words that would assure him that it wasn't the right time for her to get pregnant. She didn't want to think of how many babies she'd delivered whose mothers had thought it hadn't been the right time.

"You don't have to worry about that, Cole. If I am pregnant, I can certainly manage to take care of my baby."

He reached out and stroked the side of her face. "Our baby. You would not have gotten pregnant by yourself.

Promise me that if you discover you are, you will contact me in Texas."

She nodded. She would contact him only to let him know he would be a father because he had a right to know—if it came to that. But she would not let him fill his mind with any thoughts of obligations toward her. He hadn't forced himself on her. She had come willingly. Had gotten into his bed herself. And she had been in her right mind.

"I'll be back."

He whispered the words in her ear just before easing away from her side. She figured he was going to the bathroom and was already missing his warmth. She glanced over at the clock. It was 10 a.m. It seemed later than that. She settled under the thickness of the covers as images played across her mind of them making love. Even the thought of an unplanned pregnancy didn't bother like it probably should. She'd delivered countless babies to other women and had always yearned for a child of her own. It was a secret desire.

She felt the dip in the bed and without looking over her shoulder she knew that Cole had returned. She could feel his heat again, and as he snuggled closer and pulled her into his arms…she felt something else. His huge erection. She flipped on her back and stared up at him.

"I went and got a condom out of my wallet and put it on. You'll be protected this time."

And then he was kissing her. A part of her wanted to pull her mouth free and tell him it was okay. He didn't have to protect her. To have his baby wouldn't be so bad…

But when he deepened the kiss, she ceased thinking

at all. And when he shifted positions and slid into her, she instinctively wrapped her legs around him as erotic sensations swept through her, intensified with every stroke he made. She exulted in the feel of him inside her. It was as if this was where he was supposed to be. And moments later when her body exploded in a fire of sensual pleasure, she moaned his name over and over as waves rippled through her body.

Afterward, he pulled her close against him, held her tight in his arms and kissed her temple. For the first time in more than three years she felt total contentment.

Cole loaded the last of his luggage into the rental car the agency had brought him. The sky was clear and it was time to leave, but he would always have memories of the two days he had spent here with Patrina.

He turned around. She was standing in the doorway in her bathrobe. He had asked her not to get dressed. He wanted to remember her that way. When he saw her at his father's birthday party in a few weeks and fully clothed, that would be soon enough to stop thinking of her with only a bathrobe covering her nakedness. But he would never stop thinking of how many times they had made love, how his tongue had tasted her all over, or the moans that would pass from between her lips each and every time she came.

Inhaling deeply, he closed the trunk and walked back toward the porch. A part of him wasn't ready to go, but he knew it was something he had to do. Taking the steps slowly, he walked over to her and without saying a word he pulled her into his arms and kissed her like a soldier about to leave behind his woman before being carted off to war. She returned his kiss with a degree of passion he was getting used to. He would miss her. He would miss this.

He reluctantly pulled his mouth from hers and whispered against her moist lips. "Time for me to go."

"Will you drive more carefully this time?"

A smile touched his mouth. "Will you come to my rescue again if I don't?"

She chuckled and he felt the depth of it in his gut. "Yes. I would come to your rescue anytime, Cole Westmoreland."

She wasn't making leaving easy. He didn't say anything for a moment and then asked. "Was I a good houseguest?"

"The best. Was I a good doctor?"

"Off the charts."

He paused a moment, then added. "But I think you were an even better bedmate. It's going to be hard, the next time I see you, to not want to strip you naked. Just like it's hard as hell for me to leave now without taking you in that bedroom and making love to you one last time."

"What's stopping you?"

Patrina's question aroused him, tempted him sorely. "Because one more time won't be enough. I'd want to go on and on and on. I'd never want to leave."

Cole sighed heavily. That admission had been hard to make, but it was true. Then, feeling as if he might have said too much, true or not, he took a step back.

"Remember me," he said fiercely, fighting the urge to pull her back into his arms. Instead, he took her hand

and gave it a gentle squeeze. "You're off the shelf now, Patrina. Don't go and put yourself back up there. You're too sensual a woman for that."

He turned and headed for the car and refused to look back. At least he didn't until he was pulling into the long driveway that would take him to the main road. And when he saw her in his rearview mirror, she was still standing there. The most passionate woman he'd ever had the pleasure of meeting.

Eight

"You're definitely a welcome surprise," Casey West-moreland Quinn said. She grinned across the dinner table at her brother, who had shown up unexpectedly a few hours before.

"And you made perfect time," she added. "Had you arrived in Bozeman a few days ago you would have been met with one nasty snowstorm. Everyone's been stranded in their homes for the past couple of days."

"That couldn't have been much fun," Cole replied, trying to keep a straight face.

"We had no complaints," McKinnon Quinn said, smiling at Casey before taking a sip of his coffee.

Cole chuckled. He could read between the lines and couldn't help but be happy for his sister and the man she'd chosen to spend the rest of her life with. It was so obvious that they were in love. Casey had always been a person who believed in love, romance and all that happily-ever-after stuff, but she had become disillusioned after discovering that the storybook love story their mother had weaved for them concerning their father all those years had been a lie. Cole was glad to see that things had worked out for Casey, after all, and thanks to McKinnon, she believed in love again.

He then thought about Clint and his recent marriage to Alyssa. That, too, he thought, was definitely a love match and Cole was happy for them, as well. But while falling in love and getting married were good for some people, he had decided a long time ago he wasn't one of them.

He figured he would probably be like his uncle Sid and remain a bachelor forever. Some people did better by themselves. He liked the single life, the freedom to come and go as he pleased and not be responsible for anyone but himself. He had no problem with seeking out female companionship those times when a woman became necessary.

His thoughts shifted to Patrina and the time they had spent together. She had definitely been necessary and he was glad he'd made the decision not to mention to anyone that he'd spent the past couple of days stranded at her place. But there was the possibility she could be pregnant. He decided not to worry about anything just yet.

In the meantime, the time he had spent at her place was their secret, one he preferred not sharing with anyone, least of all his sister. The last thing he needed was for Casey—who had such a romantic heart—to get any ideas about his relationship with Patrina. Besides, given his reputation with the ladies, one his sister knew well, he didn't want her to wonder what might or might not have happened at Patrina's place.

And a lot had happened. Even now he had a tough time not remembering every single detail. He bet if he were to close his eyes he could probably still breathe in her scent.

"You want more coffee, Cole?"

Casey's question broke into his thoughts and he figured from where his thoughts were headed, it was a good thing. "No, thanks, and dinner was good."

"Thanks."

"So, how are the plans for the birthday party coming along?" he asked.

Casey smiled. "Fine. And as far as it being a surprise, Abby and I decided why bother, since Dad isn't a man you can easily pull anything over on. I can't wait to call to let him know you're here. He's going to be happy to see you."

Cole knew what she said was true. Ever since finding out he was the father of triplets, Corey had done everything within his power to forge a strong relationship with his offspring.

"There's something McKinnon and I want to tell you. We told Dad and Abby, as well as McKinnon's parents last week. I was waiting to tell you and Clint at the party."

Cole raised a curious brow. "What?"

Casey and McKinnon exchanged smiles and again Cole felt the love flowing between them. Casey looked back at Cole and said, "We're adopting a baby."

Cole couldn't help the grin that shone on his face. "That's wonderful news," he said. "Congratulations."

He knew how much the two of them wanted to become parents. He also knew that, due to a medical condition McKinnon had, they could not have children the natural way.

"Thanks." Casey beamed. "And we have Dr. Patrina Foreman to thank for this wonderful news."

Cole forced his features to remain neutral when he said, "Dr. Foreman?"

"Yes, she's the doctor who delivered little Sarah. She runs a women's clinic in town, one she helped found when she saw a need. One of her patients at the clinic, an eighteen-year-old girl, wants to give up her child as soon as it's born, but wanted to make sure the baby went to good parents. Patrina called me and McKinnon, we met with the young woman and everything has been arranged, all the legal matters taken care of. We'll be given the baby within hours of its birth."

"And when is the baby due?"

"Next month."

Cole smiled. "That's wonderful. Yes, it seems that you do owe a lot to Dr. Foreman."

"She's such a nice person," his sister went on. "I'm surprised you didn't meet her either at the party that was given for me last year or my wedding, since she was at both. She's been nominated for the Eve Award here in town. The winner will be announced later this year at a special ceremony."

"The Eve Award?" Cole asked.

"Yes, each year women are nominated and judged on their accomplishments in their community. The accomplishments must have helped improve the quality of life in the community, and with all the volunteer work she does at the clinic, Patrina has certainly done that. Her husband was sheriff here and was killed in the line of duty. I think she puts in a lot of community hours because she has a genuine desire to help people, but then I'm sure it's probably rather lonely living at that ranch by herself. She spends a lot of her free time in town at the clinic."

Cole didn't say anything as he took a sip of his coffee. He didn't want to think about how lonely Patrina was or how much spending those two days with her had meant to him. Nor did he want to recall the satisfied look on her face, after spending almost an entire night and day in bed with him.

He gave a deep sigh and decided now was the time to share his good news. It was something he hadn't told Patrina and she'd become involved with him, anyway— but only because she'd known it was an involvement that would lead nowhere. He was not looking for a serious relationship with anyone, but then, neither was she.

"I have some good news," he said. "I'm no longer a ranger. I followed Clint's lead and took an early retirement." He could tell from Casey's expression that she was surprised. She of all people knew what a dedicated ranger he'd been.

"That's wonderful, Cole," Casey said, smiling brightly at him. "What on earth will you do with all that time you're going to have on your hands?" He wasn't surprised by her question. She knew he was someone who had to stay busy or else he would get restless and ornery.

"I invested a lot of the money I made when I sold my third of the ranch to Clint. They were investments that paid off. I'm meeting with Serena Preston next week. I understand she's looking for a buyer for her helicopter business. Quade's also going to join me while I'm here. He and I are working on a business deal that involves opening several security companies around the country. We've even talked to Rico Claiborne about joining us as a partner."

Rico was a topnotch private investigator who owned a successful agency. His sister, Jessica, was married to Cole's cousin, Chase, and Rico's other sister, Savannah, was married to Durango. With the family connections, the Westmorelands considered Rico one of their own.

"Sounds like you're going to be busy."

"I plan to be," he said, and decided not to add that staying busy would be a surefire way to keep Patrina Foreman off his mind. He swallowed against the heavy lump he felt in his throat. Damn, he was missing the woman already.

He leaned back in his chair remembering how she had stood on the porch watching him drive off. She had looked beautiful with the sun slanting down on her features, emphasizing that womanly glow he had left her with. Heat fired through his veins just thinking about it, as well as remembering all they had shared. He sighed deeply. Those kinds of thoughts could land him knee-deep in trouble if he wasn't careful.

Casey interrupted his thoughts. "So how long will

you be staying with McKinnon and me before you head up the mountain to see Dad?"

Cole tried not to think how far away from Patrina being on Corey's Mountain would put him. But then, he hadn't planned on seeing her again anytime soon, anyway. He figured he wouldn't be seeing her before Corey's birthday party.

"I'm not sure," he finally said. "Probably in a couple of days. I hope the two of you don't mind the company."

McKinnon chuckled. "Not at all. Besides, I want to show you all the new horses Clint sent. They're beauties."

Later that night, Cole lay on his back with his head sunk in the thick pillow, thoughts of Patrina on his mind. He glanced over at the clock. It wasn't quite nine o'clock and it didn't take much to recall what he'd been doing around this time the previous night.

He couldn't fight the memories any longer so he closed his eyes to let them take over his mind. Images of kissing her, making love to her through the wee hours of the morning gripped him, made him hard, made him long for more of the same. But then by an unspoken agreement, what they'd shared was all there ever would be. Their paths were not to cross that way again. It had just been a moment in time.

If that was the case, why did he still desire her in every sense of the word? Even now, when he didn't want to think about her, when he didn't want to remember, he couldn't stop himself from doing so. Maybe going up on Corey's Mountain and putting distance between him and temptation was for the best.

He turned his head when he heard his cell phone. He quickly reached for it on the nightstand and flipped it open. "Hello."

"Cole, this is Quade. Have you made it to Montana yet?"

"Yes, I arrived at McKinnon and Casey's place earlier today," which in essence wasn't a lie, Cole quickly thought.

"I'm flying out of D.C. the end of the week to head that way. Have you heard from Rico?"

"No, but McKinnon mentioned he's here visiting with Durango and Savannah. A bad snowstorm has kept everyone stranded for the past couple of days. The natives are just beginning to thaw out and venture outside."

He heard Quade's chuckle. "Maybe we ought to have our heads examined for thinking about purchasing that copter service. In bad weather we'll be grounded."

"Yes, but think of all the money we'll make those days when we're in the air." Cole had done his research and had no apprehensions about the helicopter business being profitable. And with all the expansions they planned to make, he saw it as a very lucrative investment.

"I'll remind you of those words when it's thirty below zero and we're inside sitting around a roaring fire waiting for the copter's blades to defrost."

He and Quade spoke for several more minutes and Cole welcomed the conversation. It kept Patrina from intruding on his mind. But the moment the call ended, the memories were back, hitting him smack in the face, and he couldn't help wondering how much sleep he would be getting tonight.

* * *

Restless and knowing a good night's sleep was out of the question, Patrina sat up in bed and glanced at the clock. It was still fairly early, not even eleven. However, considering all the chores she'd done after Cole had left to stay busy and to keep her mind occupied, she should be sleeping like a log. But that wasn't the case. Her body felt edgy, achy with a hunger only one man could satisfy.

Cole.

Each and every time she closed her eyes he was there in her thoughts, taking over her mind and reminding her of things so intimate that she was filled with intense longing. It was recapturing all the moments she had spent with him, all the kisses they had shared, but especially when she had given her body to him….

Getting out of bed, she crossed to the window and glanced out at the full moon. She recalled what Cole had said that meant. *A full moon in April is the Seed Moon. It's the time to physically plant your seeds of desire in Mother Earth.*

Her hands immediately went to her stomach when she recalled their unprotected lovemaking. Her gaze stayed firmly locked on the full moon while she considered the possible meaning of the words Cole had spoken that night. Had it been their fate to make a baby? If she was pregnant, Cole had planted seeds of desire in her, since they definitely hadn't been seeds of love. She was smart enough to know that love had not governed their behavior for the past two days. Lust had.

Her eyes shimmered with unshed tears when she recalled the months following Perry's death when she had felt so alone. It was during those months she had regretted their decision to wait before starting a family. A child would have been something of his that would have been a part of her forever.

Patrina closed her eyes and the face she saw was no longer Perry's but Cole's. She bit her lip to stop it from trembling when she was reminded of the vow she'd made never to give her heart to another lawman. It was a vow she intended to keep. She couldn't handle the pain if anything were to happen to Cole like it had Perry.

She opened her eyes. No matter what, she would never let Cole Westmoreland have possession of her heart.

Nine

A week later

Cole glanced at the scrap of paper he held in his hand and then back at the man by his side. "How in hell did we get roped into doing this, Quade?" he asked his cousin as they got out of the truck to enter the grocery superstore.

Quade chuckled. "Mainly because this is Henrietta's day off and we weren't smart enough to get lost like McKinnon did. Hey, look at it this way—the list could have been longer. And besides, Casey's *your* sister. If anything, you should have known she was bound to put us to work sooner or later."

Cole's eyebrows drew together in a frown. "Yeah, I guess you're right, but that doesn't mean I have to like it." He grabbed a buggy and went about maneuvering it down the first aisle while glancing at the list.

"Hey, isn't that Patrina Foreman over there in the frozen-food section?"

Cole's head whipped up. Yes, that was Patrina, all right. He didn't need for her to turn all the way around to make a concrete identification. His body was already responding to the sight of her. It had been a week, but it seemed like yesterday when he had made love to her, mainly because he replayed each and every detail in his nightly dreams. He couldn't close his eyes at night without reliving the time his body had been connected to hers, thrusting in and out of her and—

"Hey, Cole. You all right?"

His gaze swiftly switched to Quade. "What makes you think I'm not?" he asked, the question coming out a little gruffer than he'd intended.

He didn't miss the way Quade's mouth quirked in a teasing smile when he said, "Mainly because I asked to see that list three times, but you were so busy staring at Patrina, you didn't hear me." Quade paused for a minute, lifted a brow and asked, "Hmm, do I detect some interest there?"

Cole's chin shot up as he shoved the list at Quade. "No."

Quade chuckled. "You spoke too soon and that was a dead giveaway."

Cole quietly cursed, refusing to let Quade bait him. But it really didn't matter when he found himself steering the buggy in Patrina's direction.

"I don't see any frozen foods on Casey's list," he heard Quade say.

Cole rolled his eyes and in doing so, barely missed knocking over a display of pastries in the middle of the aisle.

"Don't you think you need to watch where you're going?" Quade said, laughing.

Cole was about to shoot some smart remark over his shoulder to Quade when suddenly Patrina turned and her widened eyes stared straight at him. "Hello, Patrina."

From the expression on her face he could tell she was surprised to see him and he couldn't help wondering if that was good or bad. He also couldn't help wondering if her nights had been as tortured as his. He was less than five feet away and had already picked up her scent, something he knew he would never forget. She was wearing a long, white lab coat over a pair of navy slacks. She looked totally professional, but he knew firsthand that underneath her medical garb she was totally female.

"Hello, Cole." She looked past him. "Hello, Quade."

A smiling Quade came to stand by Cole's side. "Hey, Trina, how's it going?" Then without missing a beat, Quade looked at Cole and then back at her. His smile widened when he said, "I didn't know the two of you knew each other."

Cole threw Quade a sharp glance. "Patrina and I met last year at Casey's party."

"Oh, I see."

As far as Cole was concerned, his cousin saw too damn much. "Don't you want to take the buggy and finish getting the stuff on Casey's list, Quade?"

His cousin glanced at Cole and said smoothly, "Sure, why not?" Then he looked at Patrina. "You're coming to Uncle Corey's party next weekend, aren't you?"

A small smile touched her lips. "Yes, I plan to."

"Good. Then we can talk more later. I'll be seeing you."

"Goodbye, Quade."

At exactly the moment Quade and the buggy rounded the corner, Cole found himself taking a step forward. There were others around and he didn't want anyone else privy to their conversation. He glanced sideways and caught a glimpse of his reflection in the freezer's glass door. He caught a glimpse of Patrina's reflection, as well. She'd taken her tongue and given her lips a moist sweep, a gesture that always turned him on. Today was no exception. He felt it, the sexual chemistry, the charged air and electrical currents that always consumed them whenever they were in close range of each other.

"I ran into Casey last week and she told me you were here but had gone to spend a few days up on Corey's Mountain," she said.

He shifted his gaze from the glass door to her. "I was on the mountain for only a couple of days."

"Oh."

"And how have you been, Patrina?"

She met his gaze. "Fine."

"Do you have anything in particular that you want to tell me?"

He could tell from her expression that she knew what he was asking. "No," she said quickly.

He couldn't help wondering if she meant, no, she didn't have anything to tell him because it was too early to know anything or, no, she didn't have anything to tell him because she knew for certain she wasn't pregnant.

"And how have you been, Cole?"

He met her gaze and held it. "Do you want to know the truth?" he asked, his voice going low and sounding husky even to his own ears.

She evidently had an idea what he might say and nervously glanced around. "No. Not here."

"Fair enough," he conceded. "Then where? Tell me where, Patrina."

Cole watched as she licked her lips again and he felt his guts clench. The need to kiss her, take hold of that tongue with his own, was a temptation he was fighting to ignore. If she had any idea what effect seeing her lick her lips had on him, she would keep her tongue inside her mouth.

She met his gaze and he knew she had to see the desire in his eyes he wasn't trying to hide—at least not from her. He wasn't sure if Quade had seen it or not. But at the moment he didn't care.

When it seemed she didn't intend to give him an answer, he opened the glass freezer door and pretended to take something out so he could get close enough to her to whisper. "I want you."

He saw her shiver. He knew his words had been the cause. Anyone else would assume it had been the result of the blast of cold air from the freezer.

"You've had me," she finally responded.

He looked at her reflection in the freezer door, imprisoned her gaze with his own. "I want you again." And to make sure she hadn't misunderstood him, he closed

the door and turned to her. He held her gaze and repeated, "I want you, again, Patrina."

The stark determination she saw in Cole's eyes sent
another shiver up Patrina's spine. She inhaled deeply,
fought for control with all the strength she could muster.
She wanted him, too, but if she was going to stick to her
resolve, she knew what she had to do.

It wasn't that she regretted anything they'd done
when he'd been stranded at her place, but a repeat per-
formance would serve no purpose and in fact, only make
matters worse. She could barely sleep at night as it was.
If she took him up on his offer, what would happen to
her when he left Bozeman? With some people, usually
men, it was easy to replace one lover with another, but
that wasn't the case with her. Cole was the man her body
wanted. The only man it wanted. And she refused to
become addicted to something she couldn't have.

"Patrina?"

She forced even breaths past her lips, while fighting
the sexual pull between them. She had to stand firm. She
had to stay strong. She had to ignore that telltale ache
between her legs, and the tingle in her breasts.

"No, I don't think that's a good idea," she finally said
softly, making sure the words were for his ears only.

Then, simultaneously taking a deep breath and taking
a step back, she glanced at her watch and said in a
normal tone, "I didn't know how late it is. I have to go.
It was good seeing you, Cole. Tell Casey and McKinnon
I said hello."

Then she quickly swept her buggy past him, ignoring

the determined glint in his dark gaze. She could still feel the heat of that gaze on her back when she steered her buggy toward the checkout line. She was tempted to stop, turn and look him in the eye and invite him over tonight, but to do so would be foolish.

She had gotten her purchases paid for and bagged when she finally looked back. Cole was nowhere in sight, but she had a feeling she hadn't seen the last of him. She of all people knew he was a man who eventually got whatever he wanted.

"Okay, what's going on with you and Patrina?"

Cole shrugged, then turned the key in the truck's ignition and pulled out of the store's parking lot. "What makes you think there's something going on?"

Quade rolled his eyes heavenward. "Have you forgotten I'm considered one of the president's men? For years my job has been to notice things others might find irrelevant. And to pick up on things some might overlook." He smiled. "Besides, the heat between you two was so hot I was worried about the food in the freezer thawing."

"You're imagining things."

"I'd rather you told me it's none of my business than insult my intelligence."

Cole brought the truck to a stop at a traffic light and glanced at his cousin. Quade, at thirty-four a couple of years older, was the first of the Westmorelands he and Clint had met on their quest to find their father. Quade had shown up in Austin, demanding to know why they were having his uncle, Corey Westmoreland, investigated. And then, after they had given him their reasons, he had been the first one to welcome them to the Westmoreland family and the one who'd brought them to Montana to meet face-to-face the father they'd thought was dead. For that reason, the two of them shared a special bond that went beyond family relations.

He knew he couldn't tell Quade everything, but he would tell him enough, especially since he'd picked up on the vibes, anyway. Cole returned his gaze to the road when the traffic light changed and the truck began moving again. "Patrina and I are attracted to each other. Have been since that night we met last year at Casey's party."

"I picked up on that much," Quade said, shaking his head. "Tell me something I don't know."

Cole chuckled. Quade wasn't the easiest of men at times. "She prefers not getting involved with anyone in law enforcement."

"Um, last time Trina and I talked she wasn't interested in getting involved with anyone, period, lawman or otherwise."

Cole snapped his head around and gave Quade a stony look. Quade grinned. "Please keep your eyes on the road, cousin, and take off the boxing gloves. It's not that way with me and Trina. We're nothing but good friends and always have been. I've known her since she was knee-high and would see her every summer when all of us came to spend time with Uncle Corey on his mountain. She, her brother, Dale, along with McKinnon, were my playmates."

Cole nodded. He'd heard about those summers. They were times he, Clint and Casey had missed out on because his mother hadn't told them the truth.

"Why haven't you told her you're no longer a ranger?" Quade asked, breaking into his thoughts.

"Because what I do for a living shouldn't matter."

"It does and you know why. Trina and Perry had been together for years and she took his death hard. I can understand her feeling that way."

"Well, I can't. It's been more than three years and at some point she needs to get on with her life. She has a lot to offer a man. She's special. I picked up on that the night we met. I also picked up that she was standoffish where men were concerned."

"And why does that bother you so much, Cole? Could it be more than just a physical attraction you feel for her?"

Cole didn't like where Quade was going, especially when he didn't know the whole picture. Cole would be the first to admit that when they'd made love, he'd had feelings for her he'd never had with any woman before. He would go even further and admit that since that time she had become lodged in his mind and he couldn't get her out, and that although he'd told her today that he wanted her, she didn't have a clue about just how *much* he wanted her. She'd become an ache he couldn't get rid of and he didn't like it.

"Cole?"

It then occurred to him that he hadn't answered Quade's question. "It's nothing more than a physical attraction. No big deal. I'm not looking for serious involvement and I don't do well with long-distance romances. Besides, I'm a loner. I don't ever plan to get serious with a woman and marry."

"Same here. Unless…"

Cole glanced at Quade when they stopped at another traffic light. "Unless what?" he couldn't help asking.

Quade met his gaze. "Unless my path crosses again with that woman I met in Egypt a few months ago. I went over there to scope things out before the president's visit, and late one night when I couldn't sleep, I went walking on the beach. She was out walking on the beach, too."

"An Egyptian girl?"

"No, American."

Quade didn't say anything for a moment, but Cole could read between the lines. Quade and the woman had ended up spending the night together. "So…" Cole said slowly, "did you get her phone number so the two of you could stay in touch?"

Quade shook his head. "No. When I woke up the next morning she was gone. The president arrived that day so I didn't get a chance to go look for her. But believe me when I tell you that she is one woman I will never forget."

Cole nodded. He knew that no matter where *he* went in life, Patrina was the one woman he wouldn't forget, either. He also knew he would seek her out for a definitive answer to his question about her possible pregnancy. If it was too early to tell, fine, he would wait it out. But he figured that with her being a gynecologist, she had the ability to find out way ahead of most people.

He made up his mind to pay her a late-night visit. She had avoided him in the store but he wouldn't let her avoid him tonight.

* * *

When her car came to a stop at the last traffic light she would see for a while, now that she was on the outskirts of town, Patrina rubbed the back of her neck, feeling totally exhausted.

Today she had done a double duty. First she had worked eight hours at her office, and then she'd gone to the clinic where she had worked an additional eight. She hadn't intended to stay that long at the clinic, but it had been short staffed. Several women had delivered and a few other women, who had sought shelter from the blizzard, had received treatment for a few common gynecological concerns. The clinic needed money for new equipment, and she hoped the kickoff to their fund-raising drive would send some generous donors their way.

Without work to keep her mind occupied now, she couldn't help but remember running into Cole today at the store. She had volunteered to do grocery-shopping for Lila Charles during her lunch hour. Ms. Charles, who was close to eighty and lived alone, had been one of her grandmother's dearest friends. Whenever Patrina got the chance, she would stop by to check on the elderly woman and go pick up whatever items she needed from the grocery store. Cole Westmoreland had been the last person she had expected to run into there.

But she had, and it had taken everything within her to keep a level head, especially since her body had responded to him immediately. He had looked so good, but then Cole never looked anything but. He wore jeans like they'd been made exclusively for him, and a shirt that fit perfectly over the muscles of his chest.

She'd understood what he'd wanted to know. But she didn't have an answer for him yet. It would be another week or so before she did, and so far she hadn't felt any changes in her body. But it was too soon to tell.

She reached toward the car's console and pushed the CD button, deciding to listen to some music to soothe her rattled mind. She had another ten or so miles to go and decided she would let Miles Jaye, his red violin and his sexy voice relax her a bit. A short while later, she decided Miles was relaxing her too much with such romantic and heart-throbbing sounds. And the songs reminded her of cold nights wrapped up in the heated embrace of a man. Although she had listened to these songs countless times, she hadn't been able to relate to them so intensely until now. She was reminded of the time spent making love with Cole.

Even with her eyes fully opened, she could vividly recall every moment of the night and day they had spent in each other's arms. A heated shiver went up her spine when she thought of the look in his eyes just seconds before his body slid into hers and how she had stretched to receive him and the way her thighs had tightened around him and how her hips had cradled him while he moved in and out of her at such a luscious, mind-blowing rhythm and pace.

Preoccupied with those lustful memories, once she made the turn into her driveway off the main road, it took her several moments to register that a car was parked in front of her house. Once her lights shone on the vehicle, she recognized it immediately as the rental that had been delivered to Cole. Her heart skipped a beat. It was close to midnight. What was he doing here? What did he want?

Then it dawned on her just what he wanted when his words of earlier that day came back to her, and stroked her skin like a sensual caress. *I want you again, Patrina.*

She sucked in a deep breath when she brought her car to a stop. She unbuckled her seat belt and watched as Cole opened his car door and eased out of the vehicle, closed the door and then leaned against it. Waiting.

She knew she couldn't sit in her car forever; besides, she was tired, annoyed…and edgy. Boy, was she edgy. The insistent, aching throb between her legs that had been there all week just wouldn't go away.

She pulled the key from the ignition, placed her purse around her shoulder and opened the car door. The moment she did so, Cole moved toward her, forever the gentleman, and offered her his hand. She decided not to take it just yet. She watched him study her features and figured she must look a total mess, but then, who wouldn't after working sixteen hours straight?

"What are you doing here, Cole?" she asked, his height making it necessary to tilt her head back to meet his gaze.

"I didn't think we had much privacy earlier today and felt we still needed to talk."

"Well, you thought wrong. I've been at work since six this morning and—"

"Why?"

She lifted a brow. "Why what?"

"Why are you just coming home now?" he asked, his features hard.

Patrina's temper flared. "Not that it's any of your

business, but I worked at my office seeing patients and then I left there and put in another eight hours at the clinic. When you saw me today at the store I was there picking up a few items for Lila Charles, an elderly woman who was a good friend of my grandmother's. She doesn't have any family."

Thinking she'd said enough, more than he really needed to know, she sighed deeply and saw his hand was still stretched out to help her out of the car. Convinced she was only accepting his act of kindness because she was too tired to do otherwise, she took his hand.

The moment their hands touched, it happened. A shiver raced through every part of her body and she glanced up at him, hoping he hadn't felt it, too. But from the darkness of his eyes, the heated gaze, she knew that he had. Her heart skipped a beat. Then another. And another.

All sense of time was suspended as they stared at each other and finally she knew she had to say something. So she said just what she felt. "I'm tired."

She saw a softening around the edges of his gorgeous mouth and then he said in a low, throaty voice, "Of course you are, sweetheart."

She didn't have time to react to his term of endearment when, still holding her hand, he leaned down, pushed her hair aside with his other hand, then cupped the back of her neck and drew her mouth to his. She closed her eyes the moment their mouths made contact and forgot how tired she was. Instead, she felt only the way his lips were gliding over hers, the way his tongue went inside her mouth when she released a breathless sigh and the gentle way it was mating with hers. She felt her entire body respond, felt the nipples of her breasts throb with an urgency to have him touch them, take them in his mouth and taste them.

And then, without warning, she felt herself being gently pulled from the car and lifted up into his arms. As he closed the car door with his hip, she pulled her mouth away from his. "Cole, put me down. I'm too heavy."

"And I've told you before, you're not."

She sighed deeply, too exhausted from work, as well as from the effects of his kiss, to argue. Instead, she buried her face in his chest, inhaling the manly scent of him.

"Open the door, Patrina."

While still cradled in his arms, she managed to work her door key into the lock and felt the warmth of the interior of her home when he stepped over the threshold and closed the door behind them. She thought he would put her on her feet, but instead, he moved down the hall toward her bedroom.

"Now wait just a minute, Cole. How dare you assume that you can show up here tonight and think I'll sleep with you again?"

He placed her on the bed and gazed down at her. "That's not why I'm here, Patrina. I came to talk, but you're too tired. There's something else I can do, though."

He left the room and walked into the adjoining bathroom. Then, seconds after she heard the sound of water running, he reappeared in the doorway. "Your bath will be ready in a minute, so start taking off your clothes. I'll give you five minutes and if you haven't stripped down by then, I'll be more than tempted to do the honors myself." And then he disappeared again into the bathroom.

She glared at the closed bathroom door, but then thought, *Wow!* She'd never had a man run a bath for her and God knew she could use a good soak tonight. Deciding to move as quickly as she could before he made good on his threat and came back, she stripped off her clothes and slipped into her bathrobe, then pulled a short nightgown out of the dresser drawer. All in five minutes.

She turned when he opened the door again. He lifted a brow as he looked her up and down and then glanced at the pile of clothes in the middle of the floor. As if satisfied, he returned his gaze to her. "Ready?"

She nodded. "Yes."

And then he moved toward her and in one easy swoop, picked her up in his arms and headed for the bathroom. "You're going to hurt yourself if you keep doing this," she said.

"No, I'm not."

She didn't have time to argue when she felt him lowering her into the warm, sudsy water, removing her robe in the process. Part of her robe got wet, anyway, but she didn't care. He had used an ample amount of her favorite bubble bath, more than she would have, but she didn't care about that, either. At the moment she didn't want to care or worry about anything and she settled back against the tub, closed her eyes and let out an appreciative moan. The warm, sudsy water felt heavenly.

"Let me know when you're ready to get out."

She opened her eyes and looked up at Cole. He was standing at the foot of the tub. "I can get out myself."

He nodded. "I know you can, but I want you to let me know when you're ready to get out so I can help you."

She frowned and decided to take advantage of the wonderful bath he'd prepared for only a few minutes longer and get out of the tub on her own before he came back. She closed her eyes again and that was the last thing she remembered.

Cole glanced at his watch after neatly placing Patrina's clothes across the back of the chair. Her lush feminine scent was all in them, especially her undies. He forced the thought from his mind as he made his way back into the bathroom. He had expected her to call him by now, and when he eased open the door and saw her in the tub asleep, he wasn't surprised.

Taking the huge velour towel off the rack, he reached down and pulled her up into his arms. She came wide awake in that instant. "No, Cole, I can dry myself. You don't need to do this."

"Yes, I do, baby. Let me take care of you, okay," he said softly, politely.

Something in his voice must have calmed her, he thought, made her give up the protest, or it could be as he assumed. She was just plain tuckered out. He wondered how often she worked like this, pulling double hours. He then recalled what Casey had said about Patrina being up for some award for her dedicated service to the community. Now he understood why. The blasted woman needed someone to take care of her or she would work herself to death.

He went about wrapping a dripping wet Patrina up in the large towel and, after placing her on her feet, he made an attempt to dry her off. When she reached her hands down to cover her feminine mound from his view, he smiled and said, "There's no need to do that. I've seen it all before, remember?"

She removed her hands. Going down on his knees, with painstaking gentleness he began drying her, every inch of her body, and as he'd told her, every place the towel touched he had seen before. But it didn't stop him from fighting the urge to replace the towel with his hands and touch her all over, fondle her in those areas he remembered so well, those he loved caressing. And that would be every single place on her body—skin to skin, flesh to flesh. Especially those full-figure curves, voluptuous thighs and childbearing hips.

Childbearing hips.

That immediately reminded him of the reason he had sought her out tonight. Instinctively, his hand went to her stomach and his palm gently flattened against it. Something primal, possessive and elementally male clicked inside him at the thought that even now, his child could be right here inside her.

Amazing.

Leaning forward, he removed his hand and placed a kiss right there, just below her navel. It didn't matter to him if she was pregnant or not, what mattered was the possibility and the fact that he had given her a part of him no other woman could claim—his seed. Whether it hit fertile soil, only time would tell. Unless…

He glanced upward and she shook her head and said softly, "It's too early to tell, Cole. I promise that you will be the first to know."

He nodded. Satisfied.

Tossing the towel aside, he grabbed her nightgown from the vanity. "Raise your hands, Patrina," he said, trying to ignore her nakedness, especially those breasts that moved upward when she lifted her arms. They were breasts that he enjoyed putting his mouth on. He pulled down the nightie, which barely covered her hips. He immediately thought of one word to describe how she looked in it. Sexy.

He then swept her up into his arms and carried her from the bathroom into the bedroom, where he settled her on her feet. "Did you enjoy your bath?" he asked as he turned back the covers of the bed,

"Yes, and thank you."

"You're welcome."

He moved aside. "Come on, let me tuck you in."

She slid between the sheets and he pulled the blanket and spread up to cover her. "Is there anything else I can do for you?" he asked.

"No. You've done more than enough."

He grabbed the book she had placed on her nightstand and settled in the chair beside her bed. The book was the same one she had finished reading last week, the one his cousin Stone had written. "You aren't going to leave?" she asked him.

"Not until you've fallen asleep."

She nodded. "Where does your sister think you are this time of night? It's almost one in the morning."

He smiled. "She thinks I'm over at Durango's playing cards with him and Quade."

"What if she—"

"Relax, she won't." He met and held her gaze. "And if she does, will it bother you?"

She didn't hesitate. "No." Then a few seconds later, she added, "To keep it a secret was your idea, not mine. Besides, if I'm pregnant everyone is going to wonder how it happened."

His mind was suddenly filled with the memory of how it happened, all the times they'd made love. He began to get aroused. Thinking it best to steer his thoughts in another direction, he said, "Don't worry about it. I have everything under control."

A smile touched her lips before she shifted her body to a more comfortable position and closed her eyes. He sat there for a long time just staring at her, tempted to reach out and push a stray lock of hair from her face. He was tempted even further to lean over and kiss her, slide into bed with her and hold her during the night.

And like before, his feelings were intense. Feelings he'd never had for any other woman. Damn, he thought, what was happening? Those feelings shouldn't be possible for him.

He pinched the bridge of his nose and sighed deeply. He glanced over at the bed, saw the steady rise and fall of her chest and knew she had lapsed into a deep sleep.

It was time for him to leave, but he couldn't seem to force his body from the chair. So he decided to stay and watch over her for a little while longer. And the longer he sat there, the more he knew that Patrina Foreman was digging her way under his skin. He didn't like it.

Ten

"Good morning, Dr. Foreman."

Patrina glanced at her receptionist when she entered the office. Tammie Rhodes was a perky twenty-year-old who worked for her full-time while taking night classes at the university. "Good morning, Tammie. How are you this morning?"

"Great. You have a full schedule today and Ellen Cranston's husband called, claiming she's having labor pains again."

Patrina smiled as she slipped on her lab coat. "Are they real labor pains this time?" she asked, thinking of the woman who wasn't due for another two months. Last time what Ellen and her husband, Mark, thought were labor pains were nothing but a severe case of an overactive child.

Tammie grinned. "I told him it would be okay if he brought her in so we could check to make sure."

Patrina nodded as she headed toward her office. Her first patient was due in an hour. That would give her an opportunity to sit down with a cup of coffee in the privacy of her office and relive everything that happened last night with Cole. She still found it hard to believe he had been there waiting for her when she'd gotten home and then gone so far as to run a bath for her, dry her off and then tenderly tuck her into bed.

She had slept like a baby and had awakened this morning to find him gone. She'd have sworn she'd dreamed the whole thing if it hadn't been for the note he had scribbled and left on her kitchen table that read, "I'll see you later." Did that mean he would be parked outside her house when she came home again tonight?

"Oh, and you got another call, Dr. Foreman. This one personal."

Patrina turned around just seconds before entering her office and lifted a brow. "From who?"

"Cole Westmoreland."

She didn't miss the look of interest in Tammie's eyes. "Did he leave a message?"

Tammie smiled. "Yes. He told me to tell you he was taking you to lunch."

Patrina frowned. "I don't do lunch."

Tammie chuckled. "That's what I told him."

"And?"

"He said you would today."

Patrina tried to keep a straight face but wondered where Cole came off saying what she would do.

"Isn't he Durango Westmoreland's cousin? One of Corey Westmoreland's triplets?"

Tammie's question broke into Patrina's thoughts. "Yes."

Both Durango and Corey were popular around these parts, but for different reasons. Before his marriage to Savannah, Durango had been well-known among the single ladies, and Corey was a highly respected citizen of the town. Everyone knew about his mountain. And everyone knew when he'd discovered he had triplets born more than thirty years ago.

"I heard that Cole Westmoreland is good-looking," Tammie said, again breaking into Patrina's thoughts.

"Excuse me?"

Tammie's smile widened. "I said I heard that he and his brother are extremely handsome."

That was something Patrina could certainly agree with. "They are."

She studied her receptionist. "Aren't they way too old for you, not to mention that Clint is now a married man?"

Tammie laughed. "I overheard my oldest sister, Gloria, tell that to one of her girlfriends. She was working at the tuxedo-rental shop and saw them last year when they came in to get fitted for tuxes to wear at their sister's wedding."

Patrina nodded. "Well, if Cole Westmoreland calls again, please tell him I'll be too busy today to go to lunch."

"He won't be calling back. He said he wouldn't. Told me to tell you to be ready to go exactly at noon."

Patrina frowned. Cole's bossiness completely erased all his kindness of last night. Instead of saying anything else about Cole, especially to Tammie, she opened the door to her office and went inside, dismissing Cole from her mind. Or rather, she tried to, but found that she couldn't.

"Let me know the next time you decide to use me as an alibi," Durango said to his cousin as they were horseback riding on the open range. Quade had left early that morning to trek up the mountain to visit with Corey.

Cole lifted a brow. "What happened?"

"Casey showed up early this morning to visit with Savannah and made a remark that it must have been some poker game last night since you didn't get in until almost three this morning."

Durango, who was three years older than Cole, shook his head and added, "Lucky for you, Savannah went to bed early, leaving me and Quade up talking, so she had no idea whether you dropped by last night or not. So rest assured, Quade and I ended up covering your ass."

Cole smiled. "Thanks."

Durango stared at his cousin. "Any reason we needed to? Quade said he had an idea where you were but he wasn't talking."

"I appreciate that and for the moment there is a reason my ass needs covering, but how much longer that need will last, only time will tell."

Durango shook his head. "Sounds like it involves a woman. I just hope she's not married."

"She's not."

"Good."

Cole couldn't help but laugh. "Look who's talking. Everybody knows your and McKinnon's history." Durango, Quade's brother, had been the second Westmoreland that Cole and Clint had met. Upon arriving in Montana, it had been Durango who had picked up him, Clint and Quade at the airport. After spending the night at Durango's ranch, the four had made the trip up to Corey's Mountain. Once there, he and Clint had come face-to-face with the man who had fathered them, as well as another cousin, Stone, and the young woman Stone would later marry, Madison. That particular day they'd also met Madison's mother, Abby, who had just reentered Corey's life a month before. Abby was the woman who had been Corey's true love for thirty-plus years.

"According to Casey, things are falling into place for Dad's party," Cole said, as a way to change the subject.

Durango chuckled, knowing exactly what he was doing. "Yes, and it will be a pretty classy event if Abby has anything to do with it. Savannah's excited about all the Westmorelands who will start arriving next week. All of us haven't been together since Casey's wedding. Everyone couldn't make it to Clint's wedding." He shook his head. "I still can't believe he got married."

"Believe it and trust me when I say he's an extremely happy man," Cole responded.

"Hey, I know the feeling."

Cole studied his cousin and believed he really did know the feeling. All it took was a few minutes around Durango and Savannah to see just how happy they were together. Marriage definitely agreed with some people.

"McKinnon and I are meeting today for lunch at the Watering Hole. You want to join us?" Durango asked him.

Cole met his cousin's gaze and smiled. "Nope. Thanks for asking, but I've made prior lunch arrangements."

Patrina smiled while studying the new set of ultrasounds she had ordered on Ellen Cranston. Ellen and her husband had come in after Ellen had endured another sleepless night of stomach pains. Tammie had made an appointment with them to arrest their fears that Ellen was having labor pains.

Patrina had ordered a new set of ultrasounds after examining Ellen's stomach. She hadn't wanted to get the couple's hopes up regarding her suspicions until she was absolutely sure. Now she was. The Cranstons, who'd been trying to have a baby for more than five years, were having twins, something their first ultrasound hadn't shown because the little boy had been hidden behind his sister. A boy and a girl. She knew how pleased the Cranstons would be and couldn't wait to tell them the news. She reached for the phone to make the call.

Ten minutes later Patrina leaned back in her chair very pleased with her conversation with the Cranstons. Ellen and Mark had been so happy they had started crying on the phone and Patrina couldn't help but be happy for them. She then unconsciously reached down and touched her own stomach. What if *she* was pregnant? If she was, she knew her heart would know the same joy that the Cranstons were experiencing right now. There were over-the-counter ways she could find out now, but she didn't want to find out that way. Having a missed period would be sign enough, which meant she would probably know something sometime next week.

"Dr. Foreman, your noon appointment has arrived."

Patrina lifted a brow at the sound of Tammie's excited voice over the intercom. In other words, Cole was out front.

Patrina stood. "Please send him in."

No sooner had the words left her mouth than her office door opened, and Cole, looking larger than life, boldly walked in and closed the door behind him. He smiled at her and said in the sexy voice that had undone her several times, "I'm here."

Cole leaned against the closed door and stared at Patrina, and the first thought that ran through his mind was how beautiful she looked today. And when she nervously swiped her lips with her tongue, the second thought was how much he wanted to taste her. Hell, from the deep inner throb in his body, he wanted to do a lot more than that, but tasting her mouth would suffice for now.

"Hello, Cole."

"Hello, Patrina."

He moved away from the door and walked over to where she was standing beside her desk. "Did you get a good night's sleep?"

"Yes, thanks for asking, and thanks for all you did to assure that I did."

He reached out and placed his hands at her waist and met her gaze. "Thank me this way."

And then he leaned forward and captured her mouth with his. The moment his tongue mingled with hers, he heard the deep moan that came from her throat and combined with the deep groan from his own. This was more than he wanted, he thought. This was what he needed—now—in a bad way. And when she arched her body and looped her arms around his neck, he shifted his hands from her waist and placed them on the thickness of her rump to urge her even closer to the fit of him, needing for her to feel him so she would know just how aroused he was. How quickly she could turn him on.

Reluctantly, torturously, he pulled back from her mouth, but not before giving it one final, thorough sweep. "I needed that," he whispered against her moist lips.

"So did I."

He pulled back, tilted his head and gazed at her, surprised by her throaty admission. He could tell from her expression that she'd even surprised herself in making it. "Will you be going to the clinic when you leave here today?" he asked her.

She nodded. "I go to the clinic every day. I'm needed there."

It was on the tip of Cole's tongue to tell her that she was needed here where she was now, right in his arms. Instead, he said, "How late will you be staying?"

She shrugged. "Until I'm no longer needed."

"Not a good answer. I'm coming to the clinic to pick you up at eight. You can give me the address over lunch."

She lifted a brow. "Excuse me?"

He smiled. "You're excused. You're also beautiful." He then leaned in to kiss whatever words she was about to say off her lips.

* * *

Patrina glanced at the clock. It was a little past seven and the clinic wasn't nearly as busy as it had been the night before, which was a good thing since Cole had been adamant about picking her up at eight. One of the other doctors had gone home, which left only her and a staff person, which was fine.

She grabbed a cup of coffee and decided that although she would be leaving work in less than an hour, she deserved a break. Earlier, things had gotten pretty hectic but now all was calm.

Pausing at the front desk to let Julia, the night clerk, know where she'd be if things got hectic again, she strolled down the corridor that would take her to the outside patio. Upon opening the door, she pulled her jacket around her to ward off the cool breeze and recalled that this time last week the entire area had been covered in snow. Like everyone else, she hoped it was the last snowfall of the season.

She stood at the rail and looked out over the lake, remembering her lunch with Cole. He had taken her to a popular café not far from the hospital and she had to admit that she had enjoyed his company. He'd told her how the plans for his father's birthday party were coming along, and that all his cousins—most of them she knew—planned to attend. Even Delaney and Jamal would be flying in from the Middle East. They had laughed together when Cole had told her about the baby bed Thorn had built for his firstborn. It was in the shape of a motorcycle, with wheels and everything.

Then things had gotten somewhat serious when she'd

asked him to tell her about his mom. She had heard the story of how his mother hadn't told them until she'd been on her deathbed that their father was still alive. Patrina admired Cole for saying that although he wished he could have gotten to know his father a lot sooner than he had and regretted the things he'd missed out on—like the summers with everyone on Corey's Mountain—he was not angry at his mother for doing what she did. It had been her decision and he respected that.

Just from hearing him talk, Patrina knew he had been close to his mother and had loved her dearly. Cole knew how it felt to lose someone, and he also knew how it was to move on, something she hadn't been able to do—until now. But still, there was something she couldn't get past and that was the fact that Cole was a lawman. While he was on duty, upholding the law, at any time some crazy person could end his life.

For the first time since losing Perry she could admit to something she thought would never happen to her again. She had fallen in love with another man. Cole.

She knew Perry would be happy for her, for finding someone else to love and moving on with her life, but knowing what Cole did for a living, she wasn't sure if she could get on with her life with him. She would always worry about the risks he might take, and she couldn't go through that again.

Anyway, the problem was academic. Cole was not in love with her. All she was to him was a challenge.

Deciding her break time was up, Patrina headed back inside. When she reached the area where Julia was working, she smiled at the woman. Julia had a very odd look on her face and had sunk back in her chair. She regarded Patrina silently when she neared.

"Julia? Is anything wrong?"

Before Julia could answer, Patrina felt something cold and hard at the middle of her back.

"No, nothing's wrong, Doc, now that you're here," a deep male voice said close to her ear. "I need the key to your medicine cabinet."

Patrina swallowed, tried to keep her cool and slowly turned to look into the hard eyes of a young man who couldn't have been more than twenty. He was holding a gun on her. "Why do you want the key?" she asked in an even voice.

The man sneered. "Don't act stupid. You know why. I want all your drugs."

Cole was just about to round the corner to see what was keeping Patrina when he heard the man and stopped dead in his tracks. He eased back against the wall, then leaned forward and peeped around the corner. The man was holding a gun on Patrina and another woman. Intense anger, combined with stark fear, crept up Cole's spine, but he knew he had to keep a level head.

He glanced around, noticed the high ceiling, the windows whose blinds were drawn and the long hallway that led to several rooms. Given a choice, he would have preferred knowing the layout of the clinic, but he didn't have a choice. The only thing he knew was that some lunatic was holding a gun on Patrina.

He then heard the man's voice raised when Patrina tried to convince him she didn't have a key. Deciding he had to do something and quickly, he backed up and came to a closet, looked inside, grabbed a lab coat and put it on. Knowing the element of surprise was definitely not a good idea in this case, he began whistling to let everyone know he was coming and hoped and prayed that neither Patrina nor the other woman gave anything away.

Taking a deep breath, he rounded the corner and saw both Patrina and the other's woman eyes widen when they saw him. He saw the look of nervousness in the man's eyes and Cole knew more than anything he had to convince the man that he was not only a doctor, but that he was the doctor with the key.

"Oh, we have another patient," Cole said, approaching the three with a cheery smile on his face. He pretended to see the gun for the first time when the man turned toward him.

"Get over here with the others, Doc," he snapped, "and one of you has less than a minute to produce the key to the medicine cabinet."

Cole, seemingly at ease, widened his smile and said, "Oh, is that what you want? I'm the one who has it."

"Then give it to me," the man said, his attention now on Cole.

"Sure. I know not to argue with man with a gun," Cole said, retaining his smile as he slowly reached into his back pocket to pull out a set of keys.

He handed them to the man, who gave them a quick glance and frowned. He then looked back at Cole. "Hey, this is a set of car keys."

Cole shook his head. "No, they're not. Look again."

The moment the man glanced down to study the keys, Cole kicked the man in the knee at the same time as he knocked the gun from his hand. Cole was about to give him a right hook, but Patrina beat him to it. Cole finished him off by hitting him hard behind the neck, which sent him crumbling to the floor, unconscious.

"Call the police," he told the other woman who'd had the sense to keep her cool through it all. He kicked the gun farther away as he glanced down at the unconscious man. He then looked at Patrina, who was rubbing her knuckles. "Who in hell taught you to hit like that?"

"Dale. After Perry died he figured I needed to know a few moves to protect myself, since I would be living alone."

Cole nodded, grateful that her brother had had the insight to do that. "You okay?" he asked softly, crossing the room to take a look at her knuckles.

"Yes, I'm okay." Then she said in quiet tone. "You could have been killed."

He lifted his gaze and looked into her eyes. "Yeah, but then so could you," he countered.

They both glanced around when they heard Julia return. "The police are on their way," she said in an excited tone.

"Thanks," Cole said, releasing Patrina's hand to glance around. He turned back to Patrina. "Where the hell is security?"

"We haven't had security in months," the other woman answered. "Couldn't afford it. The clinic's on a tight budget."

Cole switched his gaze from Patrina to stare at the

woman, not wanting to believe what she'd said. *No security?* He was about to say something and decided not to. There was one way to remedy the problem, and he knew that after today, there would always be security protecting the clinic.

It was hours later before they were finally able to leave the clinic. That was only after law enforcement had asked questions, taken statements and made an arrest.

By the time Julia had finished telling her side of the story to the authorities and news media, Cole had become a hero and made the ten o'clock news. He received calls from Casey, Durango and his father wanting to make sure he was okay. Only Casey had a hundred questions for him since the television reporter indicated the reason he had shown up at the clinic in the first place was to pick up Dr. Patrina Foreman. So much for keeping his relationship with Patrina a secret. Now the entire town knew he was seeing her.

He glanced at Patrina and was glad they were finally on the road to her house. She hadn't said much and he couldn't help wondering what she was thinking, especially when during the police officers' questioning it came out that he was a *former* Texas Ranger. He would never forget how her eyes had met his for several pulsing moments before looking away.

He figured they needed to talk about it since she'd figured, and rightly so, that he had deliberately not told her. "Let's talk, Patrina."

She met his gaze. She gave her head a little toss and her shoulder a shrug before saying, "What about?"

"Whatever you want to talk about. Let's do it now because when we get to your place and I get you inside, talking will be the last thing on my mind."

Just like he'd known it would, intense anger appeared in her face and her eyes looked to be shooting darts. He had gotten more than a rise out of her. Now she was fighting mad. He figured if he hadn't been the one at the wheel she would probably haul off and punch him the way she'd punched the intruder.

"You arrogant ass. How dare you think when you get me home, you will do anything to me? You haven't even been honest with me. Not once did you tell me that you were no longer a ranger. You had me thinking you were still in law enforcement. Why didn't you tell me?"

"Was I supposed to?" He pulled the car off the main road and into her driveway, then parked in front of her house and turned off the ignition. Good. They would have it out now, because like he said, when they got inside they would make love, not war. He turned to face her.

"You knew how I felt," she said angrily.

"How you felt about what you *thought* was my job didn't matter to me, because sleeping with you, becoming involved with you, had nothing to do with what I did for a living. You assumed I was a Texas Ranger, yet you slept with me, anyway. Your mouth was saying one thing, but your body was saying another, Patrina. I decided to pay closer attention to what your body was saying because it truly knew what you wanted."

She stared at him and then said quietly, "You could have gotten killed tonight, Cole."

"Hey, he was holding that gun on you first, Doc. You

could have lost your life just as easily." The thought of that made his gut twist. He had come close to knocking the damn man unconscious again after the police brought him around to make an arrest.

Then in a softer voice, he said, "I could have lost you."

Releasing his seat belt, he leaned toward her. "And that's something I could not let happen."

Patrina stared deep into Cole's eyes, and then shifted her gaze to stare at his mouth. What was there about the shape and texture of it that made her want to run the tip of her tongue all over it, kiss it, get lost in it?

She tried keeping her mind on track, taking in what he'd said, noting the heartfelt way he'd said it. They were involved, at least for the moment. In another week or so he would be leaving Montana to return to Texas. Things between them would come to an end. And if she was pregnant, she would become a single parent.

One of the reasons she had made love with him was because she'd known, regardless of him being a Texas Ranger, she was only capturing a moment in time, seizing an opportunity. She hadn't been looking for anything more than that, definitely not anything lasting. He hadn't promised her that and she hadn't expected it. What they had shared had been about wants and needs, fulfilling desires, experiencing satisfaction of the most potent kind.

It was about him taking her off the shelf to live a vibrant and rewarding life, reminding her of the woman she was, of the passion she had tried so hard to ignore and hide.

"I'm going to kiss you, Patrina."

His words penetrated her mind and she met his gaze. He'd spoken with amazing calmness, deep-rooted determination and ingrained authority. He was a take-charge kind of guy. If she had any doubt about that characteristic before, she didn't now, especially after seeing how he'd handled the would-be robber.

"But that's not all I'm going to do to you," he added, inching his face even closer to hers. "We can do it out here or we can take it inside." His mouth curved into a warm smile.

His smile would be the death of her yet. It had become her weakness. She felt desire being stirred inside her. She inhaled deeply. He was making her crazy. She hadn't slept with a man in over three years and then Cole showed up, taking over her mind in red-hot pursuit. Even now she could feel her common sense tumbling.

"Patrina?"

She shifted her gaze from his mouth back to his eyes, thought for a second, then threw caution to the wind. "Let's take it inside."

Eleven

So they took it inside.

The moment they were across the threshold, Cole closed and locked the door behind them. She turned and he was right there, pulling her into his arms and taking her mouth with a hunger he knew was possible only with her. There was an instinctive need to mate with her the way a man mated with a woman he claimed as his.

Claimed as his.

Something jolted through Cole. He really didn't like the thought of that. He had never considered any woman as his. There might have been a passing fancy for one, but that was all there had ever been. However, he would be the first to admit that something with Patrina was different. He couldn't put his finger on what, but there was a difference. He didn't particularly care to know a difference existed, but at the moment, he would go with the flow. Especially when she brought some pretty hot dreams his way every night and given the fact that whenever he saw her, he immediately thought of sex, sex and more sex.

Like he was doing now.

And then there was the possibility that she could be pregnant with his child, which put a whole new spin on things. But he would concern himself with that when the time came. Something else that troubled him was the realization that it wouldn't bother him in the least if she was pregnant. Just *when* his thought process got shot to hell on an issue that monumental, he really didn't know.

The only thing he did know was that for the last seven days, he had been thinking about her nonstop. Had craved her constantly and needed intimate contact with her as much as he needed to breathe. And the urgency of his kiss, the hungry way his tongue was devouring the cavern of her mouth, was making him realize just how over the edge he was and just how uncontrollable he'd become around her.

He broke mouth contact thinking this had to stop. He immediately took possession of it again, deciding hell, no, it didn't. And this kiss was deeper than and just as thorough as the one before. And then moments later, it was she who pulled her mouth away, mainly to inhale air into her lungs. The pause gave him a chance to step back to see his handiwork. He saw how moist her lips were, how swollen, how thoroughly kissed. Seeing them touched him deeply. Just as deeply as seeing her standing there staring at him through the veil of lashes, with the dark mane of hair in disarray around her face. She looked sexier than any one woman had a right to look.

And he wanted her.

Desire, thick as anything he'd ever felt, surged through him, nipped at every vital part of his body, making him as aroused as a man could possibly get. If he didn't get out of his jeans fast, there was a chance he might damage himself in a way he didn't want to think about.

But he wanted to see Patrina naked first. "Come here, baby."

He watched her take a step closer to him, and despite her outward calm appearance, he saw the shiver that went through her body. When she came to stand directly in front of him, he whispered, "Closer."

When she took the step that made their bodies touch, he reached for the side zipper of her skirt and with the flick of his wrist he stepped back to watch it glide down her hips, leaving her clad in a full slip, bra and panties.

"I want it all off you, Patrina," he said in a low voice, reaching out and tracing his finger along the lace-trimmed V neckline of her slip and hearing the tiny catch of breath in her throat at his touch.

She took a step back and began removing every stitch covering her body. It took all the control he had not to help her, but he wanted to see her strip for him. And what he saw escalated his pulse, burgeoned his awareness of just what a beautiful, full-figured woman she was. The power of her feminine sexiness could literally bring a man to his knees. When she eased out of her panties, he groaned and his heart began racing a mile a minute. He felt himself get even harder.

"Now remove yours," she said.

Her words floated across to him like a gentle caress and she didn't have to say them twice. He unbuttoned his shirt, pulled it off his shoulders and sent it flying across the room. Then he kicked off his shoes, leaned over and pulled off his stocks. Straightening his tall frame, he pulled a condom packet out his back pocket and held it between his teeth while his hands went to the zipper of his jeans.

His gaze never left hers and with excruciating care, he eased his jeans, along with his boxer shorts, down his legs. He stepped out of them and, taking the packet from his mouth, he reached out to sweep Patrina off her feet and into his arms, kissing her like a man starved for the taste of her.

And then he was moving toward her bedroom. After placing her on the huge bed, he stood back to put on the condom, knowing she was watching him attentively the entire time. Being aware that her eyes were on him, especially that part of him, made him even more aroused, making it difficult to sheath himself in latex.

"Need my help?"

He glanced up at Patrina and couldn't help but smile at her serious expression. "Thanks, Doc, but if you were to touch me now, I might embarrass myself. I want you that much."

"Oh."

He shook his head. Sometimes he found it hard to believe that she didn't have a clue how sexy she was. "Okay, that does it," he said, finishing up and moving toward the bed. A smile tugged at the corners of his mouth. He would take pleasure in showing her once again the degree of his desire for her.

Patrina scooted to the edge of the bed, intent on showing Cole the degree of *her* desire for *him,* and was surprised that she could be so bold. But while she'd watched him put on the condom and seen his growing arousal as he did so, something deep inside her had been triggered. A desire to know him in a way she had never known any man, including Perry.

She reached out and looped her arms around Cole's neck and he pulled her closer to him. So close that she felt the tips of her breasts pressed against his hard, muscular chest. She felt secure in his arms. She felt like she was in a very special place, a place where she belonged.

She moved her hands to his shoulders and thought he felt rather tense. "Relax," she whispered softly.

"Uh, that's easy for you to say, baby. You're not the one about to come unglued."

"Wanna bet?"

And then she pushed him sideways and he tumbled on the bed with her straddling him. Cole was a take-charge man, but for once, she wanted to be in control. She gazed down at him.

"This position is different," he said, and before she could respond, he lifted his head from the pillow and captured a breast with his mouth.

The moment his mouth captured the nipple between his moist lips, she threw her head back and moaned. The man definitely had a way with his tongue. He also had a way with something else, and it was something she wanted.

But first…

She pulled back and he had no choice but to release her breast. She scooted back some to lean back on her haunches and look at him, getting a good view of him from the knees up. He evidently saw the determined glint in her eyes, saw where her attention lay while she licked her lips, and he said huskily. "I hope you're not about to do what I'm thinking."

A sweet smile touched her lips. "I don't know what you're thinking," she said, reaching out and running her hand up his inner thigh, marveling at how firm the muscles were there.

"You're trying to kill me, aren't you," he said, and she could tell the words had been forced through clenched teeth.

"No. I want to pleasure you the way you've pleasured me," she said, watching how he got even more aroused before her eyes. She suddenly felt downright giddy at the thought that she had the power to make him do that.

Her fingers began moving again, easing closer to his aroused shaft, and she could hear his sharp intake of breath the closer she got. And then she had him in her hands, and deciding she wanted to taste him and not latex, she slowly rolled the condom off him.

"Do you know how hard it was to put that damn thing on?" she heard him ask in a near growl.

"Yes, I watched you the entire time. And watching you is why I want to do this," she said, bending forward to take him into her mouth. His body jerked at the intimate contact, and she took her hands to hold down his thighs, deciding he wasn't going anywhere except where he was right now.

She tasted him the way he had done her several times that night they'd been stranded together, and felt the size of him fill her mouth. And with each circular motion she made with her tongue, with each tiny suction of her lips, she felt him gasp, felt the flat plane of his stomach tighten. She was aware of the exact moment he reached for her hair and began methodically massaging her scalp while uttering her name over and over again. She hadn't known until now how much pleasure she could bring him this way.

And then she felt his body jolt, felt his hand tugging hard, trying to pull her mouth away, but she held firm, showing him just how much staying power she had. He was left with no other choice but to shudder through it, and he cried her name, a loud piercing sound, as his body quivered uncontrollably.

After one final hard jerk of his body, she slowly released him and watched as he lay there trying to discover how to breathe again. She reached into the nightstand next to the bed and retrieved a new condom packet. Ripping it open with her teeth, she began putting it on him. He opened his eyes and met her gaze.

She shrugged and said softly, "After the last time we did this, I decided to be prepared, since I wasn't sure when you might come back."

"But you knew I would." He issued it as a statement and not a question.

"I was hoping you wouldn't. We took chances. You made me feel things I've never felt before. You made me appreciate being a woman."

"And was that a bad thing?" he asked quietly.

"No, but I hadn't wanted to feel that way again, at least not to the extent that you were forcing me to."

He didn't say anything for a few moments and then asked in a low, throaty voice, "And now?"

A smile touched her lips and she moistened those lips with her tongue. "And now I want to make love to you all night and worry about what I should or should not do tomorrow."

He shifted their bodies so that she was beneath him, looking up at him. He had gotten aroused all over again. "All night," he said, a sexy smile forming on his lips as he trailed his fingers down her cheek.

"Yes, all night."

His hand left her face and traveled low, past her stomach to settle firmly between her legs. When his fingers began stroking her, she closed her eyes as sensations began overtaking her.

"Open your eyes and look at me, Patrina."

The moment she did so, he positioned his body over her and slid into her moistness. The connection was absolute, and when he began moving in slow, thorough thrusts, she felt her body give way and began shattering into a hundred thousand pieces. Automatically, she wrapped her legs around him to hold him in.

And when she felt his body begin to shake, she knew that together they were again finding intense pleasure in each other's arms.

Hours later, the sharp ring of the telephone brought both Cole and Patrina awake. She glanced at the laminated clock on the nightstand before reaching for the phone. It was almost four in the morning. "Yes?"

She pulled herself out of Cole's arms to swing her legs over the side of the bed. "How many minutes are they apart?" Then a few seconds later she said, "I'm on my way."

"A baby decided to come now?"

She glanced over her shoulder at Cole. He had pulled himself up in the bed. "Yes, but this isn't just any baby," she said, standing, about to head to the bathroom to dress.

"Oh? And why is this kid so special?"

She turned and smiled at him. "Because it's your niece or nephew."

At his confused expression, she said, "Veronica is the eighteen-year-old girl who's giving her baby to Casey and McKinnon to adopt. The baby wasn't due for another month or so. While I'm getting dressed, give them a call and ask them to meet me at the hospital."

For as long as he lived, Cole doubted he would ever forget the look of profound happiness on his sister's face as she held her newborn son. He glanced at McKinnon, who was standing beside his wife, gazing down at the blessing they'd both been given, and knew this was a profound moment for him, as well.

"Have the two of you decided on a name?" he decided to ask to break the silence.

Casey glanced at him with tears shimmering in her eyes. "Yes, McKinnon and I wanted to honor our fathers by naming him Corey Martin Quinn."

Cole nodded, thinking the name fitted. According to

Patrina, the baby weighed almost six pounds. Cole thought he was a whopper, considering he'd been premature, with a head of curly dark hair.

He switched his gaze from the baby to Patrina when she reentered the room. "The baby will have to remain here at the hospital for another day," she said to Casey and McKinnon. "After that you'll be free to take your son home."

"How is Veronica?" Casey asked.

"She's doing fine, but she hasn't changed her mind about not wanting to see the baby. She says all she wants to do now is get on with her life, move back to Virginia and return to school."

Cole listened. From what Patrina had told him on the drive over to the hospital, the young woman, Veronica Atkins, had been someone who had dropped out of school and taken off with a member of some rock band. After she had gotten pregnant, the guy had dumped her, and with no family to call on for help, she had moved into the local Y and gotten a job at a diner. She had lived in and out of foster homes all her life and wanted something better for her child, a life with a family who would give him stability and love. She had asked Patrina if she knew of a couple who would want her child, and Patrina had immediately thought of McKinnon and Casey.

"But of course as the baby's parents, you're free to visit him as often as you want," Patrina added, smiling.

"Thanks for everything, Trina," McKinnon said, gazing lovingly at his son and his wife.

"You don't have to thank me, McKinnon. You and Casey deserve your son like he deserves the two of you." Patrina then glanced over at Cole, and Cole felt a pull in his gut. Sensations spiraled through him with mesmerizing intensity. He could picture Patrina holding a child the same way Casey was doing now.

He drew in a deep breath and his entire body seemed to tense with an awareness he had not felt until this moment. It was electrifying. It was an eye-opener and it almost made him weak in the knees. He wanted to withdraw but knew he couldn't. He had to face what was so damn clear it was unreal.

He loved her. He had fallen in love with Patrina.

Dear heaven, how did that happen? When did it happen? He knew the answer to the latter. He had fallen in love with her the very first time he had made love to her and she had trusted him enough to give her body to him after holding herself back for so long. And then when her life had been threatened and that lunatic had held a gun on her, a part of the hard casing surrounding his heart had fallen off, as well.

He wanted to cross the room and whisper how he felt and then kiss her the way a man kisses the woman he loves. But he knew he couldn't do that. Casey was already curious about what was going on. She had asked questions after the robbery attempt, but he had refused to give her any answers. She had asked questions again, just seconds before she and McKinnon had been herded off to the birthing room to be part of the delivery as Veronica had requested. She had also requested to be out during the delivery and hadn't wanted to be told anything about the child, not even if it was a boy or girl.

Inhaling deeply, Cole crossed the room to Patrina and

lightly stroked a finger down her cheek, not caring if Casey and McKinnon noticed. "Ready to go, Doc?"

She drew in a ragged breath and smiled. "In a second. I just need to clean up first and fill out a few papers."

He nodded and watched as Patrina left the room.

"What's going on, Cole? With you and Patrina?"

He met his sister's gaze. It was filled with accusations and he understood why. She knew his history when it came to women, but he wanted to assure her that this time things were different. "I love her and plan to marry her."

He could tell from the expression on Casey's face that his bold statement had been a shocker. "But how? The two of you barely know each other. You just met last year and haven't spent any time together."

"Yes, we have."

He held his sister's gaze. She seemed more confused than ever, and he knew she intended to get the full story later. She then asked softly. "Does she know how you feel?"

He smiled, tucking a stray strand of hair behind his sister's ear. "If you're asking me if I've told her yet, the answer is no. But trust me, I will."

Twelve

When Cole entered the house behind Patina and closed the door behind them, he brushed aside the thought of telling her how he felt while they were making love. He couldn't hold it inside any longer. He wanted to tell her now.

"Patrina?"

She turned from placing her medical bag on the table. "Yes?"

"We need to talk."

Patrina sighed. She had an idea what he wanted to talk about. Being at the hospital around the baby had freaked him out. It had probably hit home more so than ever that she could be pregnant and what that meant, what drastic changes there might be, what demands she might make. She knew she had to assure him that she wouldn't ask anything of him.

"If I am pregnant, you don't have to worry about me asking anything of you, Cole. You've never forced yourself on me. I knew what I was doing each and every time we made love. It was what I wanted."

She turned to walk off, but he grasped her wrist. When she looked up at him, he said in a soft, yet husky voice, "Then maybe you ought to know that I knew exactly what I was doing and it was what I wanted, as well."

Her heart contracted and she couldn't help but wonder what he meant. She didn't want to jump to conclusions, but he was looking at her intensely. "What do you mean?" she asked.

"What I mean is that if you are pregnant, I didn't intentionally set out to get you that way, but *if* you are, then I would be happy about it. I want a baby…with you."

He tightened his hold on her wrist and pulled her closer. "However," he added, "more than anything, I want you. I love you."

She stared at him for a long moment, shook her head and said, "But…but…"

"But nothing. I've never told a woman that I love her before and I don't plan on ever telling another woman again. Just you. And if I need to say it again, then that's fine. I'll say it as many times as it takes for you to believe me. I love you, Patrina. And I want to marry you, regardless of whether or not you're having my baby. It doesn't matter. I want to marry you as soon as humanly possible and live here with you."

"But…but what about Texas? You've never said you wanted to live in Bozeman."

He chuckled. "Baby, I plan to live wherever you are. You know I'm no longer a Texas Ranger. What I didn't tell you is that my uncle left me, Casey and Clint his ranch house and all the acres it sits on. Casey and I retain the rights to the land and, along with Clint, have established a foundation in my uncle's name to protect wild horses and the land is used for that. However, Casey and I sold our share of the ranch to Clint. With the money I got, I invested wisely."

When she nodded, he knew she understood that much of what he was saying. In other words, he was a very wealthy man. "Quade and I, along with Savannah's brother, Rico, are looking into setting up a security firm. Also, Quade and I are talking with Serena Preston about buying her copter service."

Patrina lifted a brow. "What will Serena do without her copter service?"

Cole shrugged. "I don't know. I understand she might be moving away. Why?"

"Curious. She was involved with Dale a year or so ago, and like a lot of other women it didn't take her long to discover that 'Heartbreaker' is his middle name."

Cole nodded and decided to get the conversation back to the two of them. "So now that you know how I feel about you, will you marry me, Patrina? I promise I will do everything within my power to make you fall in love with me, too."

"You'll be wasting your time, Cole."

At his crestfallen look, she smiled and said, "You'll

be wasting your time because I'm already in love with you. I couldn't help but admit it to myself that night when I came home totally exhausted and you took such good care of me. I love you, too."

A relieved grin split Cole's face. "And you will marry me?"

She laughed. "Yes."

"As soon as possible?"

She tilted her head. "How soon are we talking?"

"Um, before next weekend. The entire Westmoreland family is coming in for Dad's birthday party and I want to present you to everyone as my wife."

Her heart did a quick flip. "You sure? You don't want to wait until I know for certain if I'm pregnant?"

He shook his head. "Like I said, sweetheart, it doesn't matter. Besides, if you aren't pregnant this month, there's a good chance that you will be next month."

She smiled. "You really want a baby?"

He reached out and placed his hands on her waist. "Yes, I really want a baby. I didn't know how much until I saw McKinnon look down at his son. Then I knew that more than anything I want you pregnant."

Tears filled Patrina's eyes and she knew she'd been given what some people never had, what some never took advantage of. A second go-round at happiness. What she had shared with Perry those five years had been wonderful and he would always hold a special place in her heart. But she loved Cole now and more than anything she would make him a good wife.

She tilted her head up and the moment she did so, his mouth was there, claiming her lips the same way he had claimed her heart. And when she was swept off her feet, she knew exactly where he was taking her. It was just where she wanted to be—for the rest of her life.

A week later

"Wow," Casey said, smiling and looking at the huge diamond ring on Patrina's finger. "My brother evidently isn't as tight with his money as I thought. That ring is simply gorgeous."

Patrina thought so, too. Married four days, she and Cole had decided to wait until later to plan a honeymoon. They'd had a small wedding, with McKinnon's father, Judge Martin Quinn, performing the rites. Immediately afterward, she and Cole, and Clint and Alyssa—the pair had flown in for the ceremony—along with Durango and Savannah, had stood beside McKinnon and Casey, as Corey Martin was christened. Reverend Miller officiated, acknowledging with a smile the three sets of godparents.

"Lucky kid," Clint had muttered after the ceremony. He had then proceeded to announce that he and Alyssa were expecting.

Cole, standing beside Patrina, had touched her arm. They had decided not to share the news just yet that they, too, would be having a baby—close to the New Year.

"I always figured my cousin had good taste," Delaney Westmoreland Yasir said, pulling Patrina from her thoughts.

Patrina glanced up and smiled. "Thanks."

It seemed that all the Westmorelands were here on

Corey's Mountain to celebrate her father-in-law's fifty-seventh birthday. And Corey's wife, Abby, along with Casey, had made things extra-special. Patrina glanced across the room. A happy Corey Westmoreland was sitting proudly in his recliner with a grandbaby in each arm. Stone and Madison's three-month-old son, Rock, whom everyone affectionately called Rocky, and Corey's newest grandson, Corey Martin. Before his fifty-eighth birthday rolled around, Corey would have two more grandbabies to add to the mix. Patrina smiled at the thought.

She then glanced over at Alyssa, who was standing near the punch bowl talking to Clint. Whatever he'd said had made his wife smile, and Patrina thought that the two of them looked happy together. She glanced at Alyssa's stomach and thought she looked further along than three months. She wondered if perhaps Alyssa was having twins. She glanced down at her own stomach, suddenly realizing she might be faced with the same fate, since multiple births ran in the Westmoreland family. So far, only Storm's wife, Jayla, had given birth to twins.

"May I borrow my wife for a second?" Cole said, appearing before the group of women and grasping Patrina's wrist.

Without waiting for a response he pulled her away and led her outside. The air was chilly and when he pulled her into his arms, she went willingly into his warm embrace. He then leaned down and gave her a long and thorough kiss.

When he released her mouth, she smiled and looked

up at him. "Um, not that I'm complaining, but what was that for?"

He chuckled. "No reason. I just wanted to kiss you."

He then pulled her back into his arms and held her tight before saying, "Spencer and Donnay will be making an announcement in a few minutes. Ian and Brooke will be making the same announcement."

Patrina arched a brow. "About what?"

When he didn't say anything but just chuckled, she pulled back and looked at him. "More Westmoreland babies?"

Cole laughed as he nodded his head. "Yep."

She grinned. "Is that all you male Westmorelands think about? Multiplying and replenishing the earth?"

"Sounds like a good plan to me." He then reached down to tenderly caress her stomach. "How are you and Emilie doing?"

She gave him a teasing frown. "*Emery* and I are doing just fine."

A smile touched the corners of his mouth. "Yeah, whatever."

They had decided to wait until the birth of their child to find out its sex. Cole, however, thought she was having a girl and had decided to name her Emilie after his maternal grandmother. Patrina had insisted she was having a boy and that his name would be Emery.

"I'm not going to argue with you, Patrina," he said, leaning down close to her lips.

"Then don't, Cole."

And then he was kissing her again and for some reason, although she wasn't one hundred percent certain, she had a feeling she would be having an Emilie and an Emery. After all, she had gotten pregnant under a full moon in April, when Cole had planted his seeds of desire.

As far as she was concerned, just about anything was possible when you were dealing with a Westmoreland.

Epilogue

November

Five months later, the Westmorelands gathered again for two special occasions. The first was to be present when Patrina became the recipient of the Eve Award and the second was for a Westmoreland Thanksgiving. It had been decided at Corey's birthday party to return to the mountain for Thanksgiving. They had a lot to give thanks for.

Everyone now knew there would be at least two sets of twins born to Westmoreland women. Brooke would be giving birth in a month to twin boys and Patrina was also having twins. The sex of her babies was still unknown.

Cole smiled when he thought about the ongoing joke between him and Patrina. He said she was having two girls and wanted them to be named Emilie and Evelyn. She thought that because of all the activity taking place in her stomach, she was having two boys. She wanted to name them Emery and Ervin. Only time would tell and they had only a couple of more months before they found out.

A card game had been going on at his place, but everyone had decided to take a break. Clint, as well as his cousins, Thorn, Jared, Chase and Spencer, had stepped outside, but Quade had stayed in.

Cole glanced across the room to study his cousin. He had noticed lately that Quade seemed restless and wondered if his cousin's decision to retire from his job as one of the president's men had anything to do with it. He of all people knew how it was when you were used to being busy and living on the edge.

"What's this?"

Cole had gotten to his feet and was about to join the others outside when Quade's startled voice caught his attention. "What's what?"

"This."

Cole crossed the room to see what Quade was looking at. It was one of those magazines Patrina had begun subscribing to once she'd discovered she was pregnant. "It's an issue of *Pregnancy.* Patrina gets one each month."

He looked down at the magazine and then back at Quade. His cousin looked like he'd seen a ghost. "It's *her,*" Quade said in a trembling voice.

Cole glanced down again at the magazine. A very beautiful model graced the cover. He raised a brow. A very beautiful and very *pregnant* model. Hell, she looked like she would be having the baby any minute. And Cole quickly canned the thought that the woman would be having one baby. Her stomach was bigger than Patrina's.

His gaze moved from her stomach back to her face. Forget about her being beautiful, she was knockout, drag-down gorgeous. And the outfit she was wearing made her look too stunning to be real. There was no doubt in his mind she was a model and probably married to some movie star.

He cleared his throat and glanced at Quade. "So you think you know her?"

Quade nodded slowly as he continued to stare at the cover of the magazine. "Yes, I know her. I met her earlier this year in Egypt."

It took Cole only a second to put two and two together. "That's her? The woman you met on the beach that night?"

Quade didn't say anything for a minute and then, "Yes, that's her."

Cole stated the obvious. "She's pregnant."

"Yeah."

"And it looks like she's having twins," Cole muttered. Looking at the cover again, he said, "I take that back. Looks like she's having triplets. Or quadruplets. And whatever she's having looks like she's having it any day now."

"What issue is this?" Quade asked, scanning the cover. Moments later he answered his own question. "It's last month's issue, which means she's probably delivered by now."

Cole nodded. "I would think so." He stared at his cousin. "So, tell me, Quade. You think you're responsible for her condition?"

Quade met his gaze. "Considering everything that happened that night, I would say yes, there's a damn good chance I am."

"Okay. And what are you going to do about it?"

Quade placed the magazine back on the table. "First I'm going to find her. And if I'm the father of her baby… or babies, then a wedding will be in order."

"And if the lady doesn't agree?"

Quade was already moving toward the guest bedroom, no doubt to pack and be on his way. "Doesn't matter. We're getting married."

When he disappeared around the corner, Cole picked up the magazine and studied the picture of the gorgeous, pregnant woman once more and said, "I don't know your name, sweetheart, but I just hope you're ready for the likes of a determined Quade Westmoreland."

* * * * *

*Don't miss Quade Westmoreland's story
this December
from Silhouette Desire.*

The editors at Harlequin Blaze have never been afraid to push the limits—tempting readers with the forbidden, whetting their appetites with a wide variety of story lines. But now we're breaking the final barrier—the time barrier.

In July, watch for BOUND TO PLEASE by fan favorite Hope Tarr, Harlequin Blaze's first ever *historical romance*—a story that's truly Blaze-worthy in every sense.

Here's a sneak peek…

Brianna stretched out beside Ewan, languid as a cat, and promptly fell asleep. Midday sunshine streamed into the chamber, bathing her lovely, long-limbed body in golden light, the sea-scented breeze wafting inside to dry the damp red-gold tendrils curling about her flushed face. Propping himself up on one elbow, Ewan slid his gaze over her. She looked beautiful and whole, satisfied and sated and altogether happier than he had so far seen her. A slight smile curved her beautiful lips as though she must be in the midst of a lovely dream. She'd molded her lush, lovely body to his and laid her head in the curve of his shoulder and settled in to sleep beside him. For the longest while he lay there turned toward her, content to watch her sleep, at near-perfect peace.

Not wholly perfect, for she had yet to answer his marriage proposal. Still, she wanted to make a baby with him, and Ewan no longer viewed her plan as the travesty he once had. He wanted children—sons to carry on after him, though a bonny little daughter with flame-colored hair would be nice, too. But he also wanted more than to simply plant his seed and be on his way. He wanted to lie beside Brianna night upon night as she increased, rub soothing unguents into the swell of her belly, knead the ache from her back and make slow, gentle love to her. He wanted to hold his newly born child in his arms and look down into Brianna's tired but radiant face and blot the perspiration from her brow and be a husband to her in every way.

He gave her a gentle nudge. "Brie?"

"Hmm?"

She rolled onto her side and he captured her against his chest. One arm wrapped about her waist, he bent to her ear and asked, "Do you think we might have just made a baby?"

Her eyes remained closed, but he felt her tense against him. "I don't know. We'll have to wait and see."

He stroked his hand over the flat plane of her belly. "You're so small and tight it's hard to imagine you increasing."

"All women increase no matter how large or small they start out. I may not grow big as a croft, but I'll be big enough, though I have hopes I may not waddle like a duck, at least not too badly."

The reference to his fair-day teasing was not lost on him. He grinned. "Brianna MacLeod grown so large she must sit still for once in her life. I'll need the proof of my own eyes to believe it."

Despite their banter, he felt his spirits dip. Assuming they were so blessed, he wouldn't have the chance to see her thus. By then he would be long gone, restored to his clan according to the sad bargain they'd struck. He opened his mouth to ask her to marry him again and then clamped it closed, not wanting to spoil the moment, but the unspoken words weighed like a millstone on his heart.

The damnable bargain they'd struck was proving to be a devil's pact indeed.

* * * * *

Will these two star-crossed lovers find
their sexily-ever-after?
Find out in BOUND TO PLEASE by Hope Tarr,
available in July
wherever Harlequin® Blaze™ books are sold.

Silhouette

Desire

HIGH-SOCIETY
SECRET PREGNANCY

Park Avenue Scandals

Self-made millionaire Max Rolland had given
up on love until he meets socialite fundraiser
Julia Prentice. After their encounter Julia finds
herself pregnant, but a mysterious blackmailer
threatens to use this surprise pregnancy and ruin
his reputation. Max must decide whether to turn
his back on the woman carrying his child or risk
everything, including his heart....

**Don't miss the next installment of
the Park Avenue Scandals series—
Front Page Engagement
by Laura Wright—
coming in August 2008
from Silhouette Desire!**

Always Powerful, Passionate and Provocative.

REQUEST YOUR FREE BOOKS!

2 FREE NOVELS
PLUS 2
FREE GIFTS!

Silhouette®

Desire®

Passionate, Powerful, Provocative!

YES! Please send me 2 FREE Silhouette Desire® novels and my 2 FREE gifts (gifts are worth about $10). After receiving them, if I don't wish to receive any more books, I can return the shipping statement marked "cancel". If I don't cancel, I will receive 6 brand-new novels every month and be billed just $4.05 per book in the U.S. or $4.74 per book in Canada, plus 25¢ shipping and handling per book and applicable taxes, if any*. That's a savings of almost 15% off the cover price! I understand that accepting the 2 free books and gifts places me under no obligation to buy anything. I can always return a shipment and cancel at any time. Even if I never buy another book, the two free books and gifts are mine to keep forever.

225 SDN ERVX 326 SDN ERVM

Name	(PLEASE PRINT)
Address	Apt. #
City	State/Prov.	Zip/Postal Code

Signature (if under 18, a parent or guardian must sign)

Mail to the **Silhouette Reader Service:**
IN U.S.A.: P.O. Box 1867, Buffalo, NY 14240-1867
IN CANADA: P.O. Box 609, Fort Erie, Ontario L2A 5X3

Not valid to current subscribers of Silhouette Desire books.

Want to try two free books from another line?
Call 1-800-873-8635 or visit www.morefreebooks.com.

* Terms and prices subject to change without notice. N.Y. residents add applicable sales tax. Canadian residents will be charged applicable provincial taxes and GST. Offer not valid in Quebec. This offer is limited to one order per household. All orders subject to approval. Credit or debit balances in a customer's account(s) may be offset by any other outstanding balance owed by or to the customer. Please allow 4 to 6 weeks for delivery. Offer available while quantities last.

Your Privacy: Silhouette Books is committed to protecting your privacy. Our Privacy Policy is available online at www.eHarlequin.com or upon request from the Reader Service. From time to time we make our lists of customers available to reputable third parties who may have a product or service of interest to you. If you would prefer we not share your name and address, please check here. ☐

SDES08R

▼ *Silhouette*®

SPECIAL EDITION™

NEW YORK TIMES BESTSELLING AUTHOR

DIANA PALMER

A brand-new Long, Tall Texans novel

HEART OF STONE

Feeling unwanted and unloved, Keely returns
to Jacobsville and to Boone Sinclair, a rancher
troubled by his own past. Boone has always
seemed reserved, but now Keely discovers a
sensuality with him that quickly turns to love. Can
they each see past their own scars to let love in?

*Available September 2008
wherever you buy books.*

COMING NEXT MONTH

#1879 HIGH-SOCIETY SECRET PREGNANCY—Maureen Child
Park Avenue Scandals
With her shocking pregnancy about to be leaked to the press, she has no choice but to marry the millionaire with whom she spent one passionate night.

#1880 DANTE'S WEDDING DECEPTION—Day Leclaire
The Dante Legacy
He'd lied and said he was her loving husband. For this Dante bachelor had to discover the truth behind the woman claiming to have lost her memory.

#1881 BOUND BY THE KINCAID BABY—Emilie Rose
The Payback Affairs
A will and an orphaned infant had brought them together. Now they had to decide if passion would tear them apart.

#1882 BILLIONAIRE'S FAVORITE FANTASY—Jan Colley
She'd unknowingly slept with her boss! And now the billionaire businessman had no intention of letting her get away.

#1883 THE CEO TAKES A WIFE—Maxine Sullivan
With only twelve months to produce an heir it was imperative he find the perfect bride...no matter what the consequences!

#1884 THE DESERT LORD'S BRIDE—Olivia Gates
Throne of Judar
The marriage had been arranged. And their attraction, unexpected. But would the heir to the throne choose the crown over the woman in his bed?

SDCNM0608